Unconcerned about the others, Tresa focused on the blonde-haired man and positioned the scythe in preparation to swing. Her intent was to decapitate Ned, the bastard she once knew as Jurgen, but she didn't expect it to happen. The blade couldn't hurt a body on the physical plane since it existed on a spiritual one. Still, her hope was her assault would do some kind of damage. She shifted her hands and caught the man's attention.

His blue-eyed gaze widened in surprise. His skin paled to match the church several yards away. *Tresa?*

Her name whispered in her mind, a soft caress she hadn't experienced since she had been transformed into the Grim Reaper. For a brief moment she considered dropping her weapon but didn't. She had waited lifetimes to inflict her revenge, to repay him for the hurt he had caused her. She smirked. *Hello, Jurgen.* The blade swung down and sliced through his neck.

The following story is a work of fiction. All names, characters, and places are products of the author's imagination or are used in a fictitious manner. Any resemblance, including but not limited, to actual events, locales, organizations, or persons, living or dead, is entirely coincidental.

DEDICATION

A big thank you to my author friend and editor, Erin S, who helped me out with the original versions of these stories (Holiday Spirits, In the Spirit and The Decision). I'd also like to say thank you to Erin Sinclair, Johanna Riley, RM Sotera & Shannan Albright for being in my life. Your friendships are appreciated more than you know! And, as always, my heart and gratitude to CJM, whose love and support of my goals keeps me going. I'm glad fate brought us all together!

~ C.R. Moss

FATE'S DEAL

~ A Collection of Three Stories ~

C.R. Moss

Hello,

I am Lady Tyche. My name is pronounced *TIE-key*, and you may know me as the goddess of fortune, Fortuna, or the personification of luck. Some may like me and others hate me, both sides, though, have said *fate's a funny thing*. Closely tied to the wheel of fortune, I am known to bring good luck or bad to a spinner's life. It is one place where I allow my capricious nature to roam free and help to determine one's life path.

Today I am here to share with you three stories of the lives I've touched.

Yours,

Fate

Fortune, good night, smile once more; turn thy wheel!
~ Shakespeare – King Lear, *The Tragedy of King Lear*,
England, 1604–1605

I know how Fortune is ever most friendly and alluring to
those whom she strives to deceive, until she overwhelms them
with grief beyond bearing, by deserting them when least
expected … Are you trying to stay the force of her turning
wheel? Ah! dull-witted mortal, if Fortune begin to stay still,
she is no longer Fortune.
~ Boethius, Consolation of Philosophy, AD 524

Lover's Fate

Chapter One

The bum. The lousy ingrate. All that time and preparation, and she copped out of running the marathon!

That Jenna's thoughts whirled with issues other than what she needed to focus on irked the bloody hell out of her. She bounced on the balls of her feet, stared up at the dark morning sky that lay beyond the bright, temporary street lamps, and blew hot, moist air into her gloved, but still freezing cold, cupped hands. Current hits from various music genres blared from the speakers that had been set up on tall stands along the perimeter of the casino's parking lot, but the loud music and noise of the growing crowd at the south end of Las Vegas Boulevard couldn't quiet her mind.

The annoying buzz of the alarm had woken her at four. She'd nervously prepped herself with the appropriate clothing, small water bottles and strategically placed packs of goo, a wonderful pudding-like substance that would give her bursts of nutrition during the race. A few times during her preparation she'd tried to rouse her friend, Katie, from her slumber so she could get ready as well, but the woman hadn't wanted to budge. The first time she'd shaken her, Katie had rolled over and said, "It's way too early." The second time she'd nudged her friend, Katie griped, "I'm tired. The flight yesterday did me in." The third time, she pulled the sheets off the sleeping woman in a flurry of impatience. Katie finally sat up, grabbed the sheets from her and flopped on the bed complaining about how cold it would be.

It was a good thing for her that her stomach had flip-flopped and churned, distracted herself from her friend's whining. Otherwise, Jenna believed she'd have woken the entire hotel with an overly boisterous and irate rant.

When she came to realize the nitty-gritty of the situation, she couldn't blame Katie for cutting out on the race. Between the two of them, Jenna was the serious one about running the marathon, getting up two hours before she normally had to for work to run in the heat and humidity, the cold, the rain, the snow. Katie joined her when she could, but hadn't trained as long and hard as she had. Katie wasn't ready. She was...or so she thought. The way her nerves zinged around her body and how her stomach clenched on the small bowl of oatmeal she'd eaten an hour ago made her think differently.

People thought she was crazy when she decided to participate in a marathon. Maybe she was. But unrequited love does that to a girl. She'd been a casual jogger. The kind of runner who went out and pounded pavement for two or three miles to work off the occasional burgers and fries, but that was it. Her interest in picking up speed came after Don, a co-professor at the university where she taught, and she had finally called it quits. Jenna had dated on and off for several years, but never felt close to him, never been able to give her full heart and soul to him. During her long training runs, she found her fear of commitment to him had stemmed from the fact that he couldn't keep his dick out of other women. Though the split had been mutual, the break still hurt. She'd decided to lose herself in running. Now here she was about ready to face twenty-six and two-tenths miles for the first time. People told her this event would change her, change her life. She planned to use the several hours of solitude to figure out if she was running from something or to something.

"Ow!" Her hand shot to her spine. She spun to see who had jabbed her back with an elbow and found herself gazing up at pair of sinfully deep dark eyes. Suddenly an urge for a slice of black forest chocolate cake consumed her.

"Ah, *scusa.*"

The tall and very well-toned gentleman placed a hand on her upper arm. An image of being held in his embrace in an enormous, plush white bed surrounded by full, fluffy white pillows, their naked skin against each other in post-coital bliss, shook her to her core. In her vision, she looked into his beautiful eyes and, in Italian, pleaded with him not to leave.

She shook her head to stop the scene from playing out and yanked her arm away from the stranger.

He leaned toward her and whispered, "Please accept my apologies. I did not mean to bump you. All these people are a bit crushing, are they not?"

"It's all right." The words, contradictory to the ire over the situation that plagued her mind, passed her lips without thought. His rich accent had rolled off his tongue straight into her ear and lapped at the edge of her awareness so gently that a sense of calm washed over her, filling her with much welcomed peace.

Her mind cleared. She stepped back and assessed the handsome stranger. He dressed in a pair of black baggy running shorts with black compression shorts poking out an inch from underneath, as if the temperature was already in the sixties and not in the low forties. The white bib with his number on it stood out, a glaring contrast against his black and white sleeveless running shirt. He had a great pair of muscled long legs and a nice set of arms too — a runner's body with meat. Again she gazed at his face, taking in his short dark curls, his sexy eyes, the strong squared chin with a bit of a cleft. His features reminded her of the classic Roman male statues she studied in her doctorate program.

"Aren't you cold?" She pitched her voice to be heard over the throng of the crowd, which had grown to immense proportions. All the runners stood shoulder to shoulder vying for a better spot to start the race. The jostling of all the bodies on the street was like leaving a sporting event — one big mass slowly moving in the same direction.

He shook his head. Jenna stared at him in surprise. She was almost as cold as she was back home running in twenty degree weather in the snow even though she was dressed in her racing clothes, sweatpants and a sweatshirt bought specifically for the race. He must have gotten the same story she had from friends and family. That, since it was Las Vegas, it'd be warm, even in December. They had been partly right. The temps did feel warm between the hours of noon and two, but not at the butt crack of dawn. Then again, she did feel warmer in the midst of the crowd than she had back at the port-o-potties while standing in line waiting to relieve herself.

"My name is Artim."

He smiled, flashing beautiful straight white teeth from behind his sexy crimson lips. Once more a wave of tranquility flowed through her as if he'd stroked her soul in a loving caress.

"I'm Jenna." She returned his smile and held out her hand. When he took it and brought it to his lips, placing a gentleman's kiss on her knuckles, her nerves pranced not with pre-race jitters, but with deep, long forgotten desire. She gazed into the depths of his stunning eyes and sighed like a lovesick school girl. No man, with just a look, had ever ignited her passion so quickly, so strongly. The throbbing want to taste and touch the texture of his skin, brush the tips of her fingers along the contours of his muscles and follow with her tongue overwhelmed her. The area between her legs, which hadn't been touched in months, moistened, pulsated in need.

"You!"

Her head whipped toward the new voice which had yanked her out of her sexual reverie. Her hand jerked from Artim's. A blonde-haired, blue-eyed man with striking Germanic features and a build similar to Artim's stood a little too close to her new attraction. The blonde's hand possessively gripped Artim's shoulder.

"Ned, be nice to my new friend Jenna." Artim jabbed the man in his side with an elbow.

Before she could question what the new guy meant by his exclamation, a thunderous boom exploded over the crowd and lit the pre-dawn sky with sparkling and sizzling color. The hulking mass pressed toward the start line. There was no way she'd be able to shout her inquiries above the roar of applause, the cheering from the sidelines and the slapping of soles on the pavement. So as not to get tripped up, she turned from the two men, faced the race course and joined the crowd in the slow walk. Jenna tried not to panic, reminding herself that once the people dispersed and everyone found their groove, the snail's pace start wouldn't matter and wouldn't affect her running time. At least that's what all the training books had said.

As Jenna focused on her breathing and quelled the urge to break out of the gate like an excited thoroughbred, she discerned Artim and Ned each taking a side. Artim grazed her right arm and a comforting sereneness filled her. All the anxiety about the race and agitation over her lazy friend broke apart and floated away.

"Thanks for keeping me company." She glanced at him with a smile.

"*Prego.*"

The bright blues, greens, reds and silvers of the flashing fireworks in the sky lit their way through the starting gate. City officials had closed off the southbound side of Las Vegas Boulevard for the Las Vegas Marathon. With a giddiness she hadn't experienced in years, she couldn't wait to see the colorful neon lights of The Strip for the first four miles. The crowd thinned, and she picked up her pace to a jog.

Ned nudged her left arm with his elbow. "What do you plan to run this course in?"

"I'd be happy breaking five hours."

"What made you decide to pound your body for twenty some miles?" Artim's deep, rich accented voice rolled on her right. He pointed at the light shooting from the top of the pyramid and rattled off words in Italian to Ned.

She sighed, remembering Don's last confession that had led to their recent and final breakup. He had admitted to sleeping with his assistant, a cute little red-headed grad student, and she'd realized he was slime. She didn't want to be with him anymore, yet still felt like a worthless clod, someone who needed to validate herself in some fashion, to remind herself she was a strong woman who could do anything. But a marathon? Even she questioned her sanity.

"A momentary lapse of reason after breaking up with a co-worker," Jenna replied.

Ned nodded.

She turned her head toward him. "What did you mean when you saw me and said 'you'?"

His sharp crystal blue-eyed glare cut into her. Artim barked a few curt Italian phrases. Ned shrugged and ran ahead several yards.

Jenna picked up her pace to an easy thirteen minutes per mile. Artim followed suit.

"What about you two?" Jenna changed the subject. She couldn't worry about what Ned thought, and it wouldn't do to let the guy's negativity get to her. She needed to stay positive.

"For this grand parade." Artim swept an arm out indicating all the runners. "For the festive atmosphere and merry-making." He waved an arm at the tall casinos and their advertising screens flashing colorful displays of shows, restaurants and games. "It's a place to celebrate the holiday season with great enthusiasm and not be chastised for it."

"Oh, like Saturnalia."

He turned toward her with a surprised expression. "You know about that?"

"Yes. That and other ancient holidays were part of my studies for history. I teach ancient religions and mythologies at the university back home."

"Interesting." Ned had slowed his pace, and they'd caught up. His flat statement was barely audible.

She gave him a quick glare of her own, not appreciating the disapproval emanating from him, nor his interruption of her conversation with Artim. If they were a package deal, she didn't know if she wanted any part of it. For now, she just needed to run.

"Well, fellas, it's been nice chatting with you, but if I want to hit my goal, I need to concentrate."

"No problem. We will see you at the end."

As the two men pulled away, she could have sworn she heard Artim say she wasn't alone anymore. She fought the impulse to join them in their faster pace to find out. The speed she had to race at needed to be slower if she wanted to make sure she was going to finish the marathon.

Then again, if she could keep close to them and hang back a few lengths, she'd have a nice view of Artim's tight ass to keep her entertained.

Chapter Two

*E*ven though she lost her view, the first seven miles were entertainment in themselves. Crowds, braving the early morning cold, lined the street and cheered the runners. The sun rose casting a golden hue on the casinos and created the illusion that the neon signs had dimmed in their colorful intensity, reducing the awe of the eye candy. The runners were enjoyable, too. A handful dressed as Santa, sans the extra padding. Others dressed in wedding garb for the run-through ceremony to be performed later, and several Elvis runners, all dressed in the famous white suit, ran scattered throughout the crowd.

Before it seemed any time had passed, she had discarded the sweatshirt and sweatpants. The throw away clothes, discarded by runners when they became hot from running, would be picked up by the race volunteers and donated to local goodwill agencies. Her racing shirt and shorts were the only items of clothing left on her body to protect her from the elements. She had passed all the sights of The Strip and Downtown and was just over an hour in to the race when, at the mile seven aid station, she grabbed a cup of sports drink from a volunteer. Jenna downed the liquid and tossed the cup as she kept moving. A little farther ahead, she spied Artim and Ned, waiting for her. She approached them, and they fell into pace beside her.

"It is said the next few miles are in a bad section of town."

She nodded as Artim's tenor voice slipped over her in a tender blanket of sound, making her want to cuddle up next to him.

"I will protect you."

I will protect you. His words resounded in her mind in a pleasing ripple of *déjà vu*, awakening a strange memory of a stroll down a gray cobblestone street in a different time.

The memory was of a market day…

Young versions of her and Artim, respectively clad in the off-white Roman apparels of a *peplos* and toga, strolled along with the rest of the crowd, stopping occasionally to examine the goods and produce of the vendors. She paused at one cart displaying various shades and textures of white cloth. Her fingers grazed a soft length of delicately woven material. She turned to her companion, presenting the cloth over her outstretched hand. "I shall have mother buy me this, craft a robe and dress me in it for our wedding."

"Whatever your heart desires, Vespasia, my love, will be yours."

He brought her other hand, which he'd been holding during the walk, up to his lips and kissed the backs of her fingers. The thick silver band on her ring finger glinted in the afternoon sun. A delighted smile twitched her lips. The public consent to their marriage to make their union official had been shown quite adequately, since not only had her love held her hand as he walked her along the street, he had kissed it as well.

"My heart desires you and only you my dear, Quintus. June will not come fast enough."

"*Sic*, my love, I agree, but once it does and you are mine, I will protect you always and keep you forever close to my heart."

"Promise?" She continued to gaze into the eyes of her love. Her core filled with a fierce longing for him.

"Promise." He stroked the backs of her fingers with his thumb.

Hand in hand they continued their promenade through the center of town, their leather sandals quietly padding the dirt

and stones beneath their feet. She and her love passed by
several small sand-colored buildings where plebes and
freedmen lived and worked, then stopped outside a grand
building with a white marble façade, steps and tall columns. It
was the place where the Senate regularly met. She squeezed
his hand, thinking how good a match they were, he a Senator's
son, and her another Senator's daughter. If only he weren't
involved with that religious cult.

"Jenna?"
The snap of fingers cracked beside her ear.
"Jenna?"
She abruptly turned toward the noise, then stumbled.
Artim grabbed her arm in gentle strength to keep her from
crashing to the ground. His graceful fingers lightly grasped her
arm as she righted myself and continued moving. The touch
of his hand, though delicate, seared her, heating her desire to a
low boil. Every nerve in her body sizzled. She wanted the
classically handsome man with an intensity she'd never known
before. The instantaneous attraction to him alarmed her. One
part of her as a scholar, who looked at the world with an
analytical mind, realized the sudden appeal to him was merely
physical, a chemical transference of sight and smell. Her other
side, as a woman and a romantic, finally understood what the
Greeks meant by *theia mania*—madness from the gods. Falling
in love at first sight, being hit with Cupid's arrow, was nuts.
And she was mad, crazy to be out in the morning cold,
running for several hours, and crushing on a man who she
knew nothing about.

"I'm all right." She sidestepped to put some distance
between them and to move away from his alluring touch. "I
got into my…um…zone and…um…lost in thought." Jenna
sensed he didn't believe her and wanted to question her
further so she held up her hand. "I'm fine, really."

"If you say so. Would you mind if I went ahead to catch
up with Ned? I believe he's feeling a little out of sorts."

The concern in his voice for her and his friend twanged at her heart strings. Artim was such a nice man, a good soul. But, how she knew that, she couldn't explain. "No, I don't mind." The words came out clipped, breathless. "I need to adjust my speed anyway. I've been running a little fast for my taste."

Artim nodded and sprinted away as if he hadn't been running for over an hour and a half.

A mile later she realized she missed having the company while she pounded the pavement. Being with someone, whether you talked or not, made the miles and time roll by faster. She couldn't dwell on being alone though. She had to keep the end in mind, the goal of finishing set firmly in front of her. Jenna had to prove to herself that, just because a guy she'd dated on and off for over ten years didn't want her anymore, didn't mean she was a washed up old hag. She had a great body, finely-toned and tuned from training for the marathon. Her sun-touched, lightly tanned skin was firmer, more radiant due to her better eating habits. Her long chocolate and caramel colored hair was fuller, shinier and silkier. Granted, the color and the shiny silky part could be contributed to her favorite hairstylist and her talent with dyes, highlights and conditioners, but still, her locks received great compliments. What did those twits, those *grad students*, who he kept hooking up with and who lived on sodas and processed foods, have over her?

Her sneakers slapped the road as she envisioned stepping on Don's head with each movement of her legs. The scenery whizzed by her. The houses and subdivisions looked different with each block. One moment she ran past beautiful homes behind concrete walls and in the next she passed what appeared to be homes built before Las Vegas became a hot spot. Then the next turn revealed not-so-well kept apartments. Talk about a melting pot. If she weren't so heavily involved in the ancient Greece and Rome projects for her classes, she'd check out the history of the interesting town. But she had enough on her plate as it was with her committees, the classes she taught and the book she had to finish to make tenure.

The book. Damn it to all hell.

Don had her notes. As a colleague, he had offered to review them for accuracy and double check her research, and when she'd handed them over, she hadn't thought twice about it. But now she didn't trust him worth a damn. The retrieval of her notes would be the first item on her agenda when she returned home. Jenna didn't want that ass to have any part of her life, colleague or not.

A cheer rang out from a crowd that had gathered on a street corner. Their calls of encouragement lifted her emotions and stopped her negative line of thinking. She waved to them and received a round of applause.

She finally understood how and why people became hooked on racing. There was the adrenaline rush, the inspiration and support from the volunteers and the crowds, and the pride from accomplishing such a lofty goal. A smile brightened her face, but the moment she came upon the next aid booth the excitement drained from her like someone had pulled the plug on a tub full of water.

Mile seventeen? I'm only at mile seventeen?

Jenna snatched a pack of goo from her race belt and consumed the warm, sticky content. She couldn't be hitting The Wall, not yet. It was too soon to burn out. Two of her training runs had taken her over twenty miles, so why was she hit with fatigue and unsteadiness at this mile? She took a deep breath and realized she'd let herself worry about a situation that wasn't in her control. *Damn.* Why did she let thoughts about Don take over? She needed to relax.

If only my friend, or Artim, were here to take my mind off the miles and my psychological hitch.

Artim. He was someone she could definitely relax with in more ways than one, even though being near him conjured up the craziest sensual images she'd ever had. And why not hook up with him? He'd be an early Christmas present to her, from her.

Artim joined her a few paces after mile eighteen.

"Are you faring well?"

His wonderfully sexy voice was like a soothing balm on her tired muscles. A supply of energy welled within her.

"I am now." Hearing the flirtatious twinge in her voice, she cringed. Still she was happy Santa had heard her wish and granted her an early gift.

"I am glad to hear it." He matched her slower stride with ease.

"You didn't have to wait for me you know. I'm sure you have your own goal you want to meet. How's Ned by the way?" She glanced in Artim's direction. The man looked fresh and vibrant. She made a mental note to ask him after the race when she wouldn't be so focused on putting one foot in front of the other what his secret was to keeping cool.

"*Sì*, I have a goal, but not to worry. Ned is fine. I keep you company for now."

"Thanks." She grazed his arm with the palm of her hand in a friendly, playful way and another image from the past flashed on her mind's screen.

It was still market day. They had snuck away from the confines of the town's center, the eyes of the marketers and patrons, and had walked out toward the hills and his uncle's vineyard. They sat on a grassy slope before the edge of the road in front of the yard. The young man put his arm around her and brought her close, drawing her into the folds of his embrace. She laid her head upon his chest, listened to the strong, slow thumps of his heart and breathed in the scent of his leather and musk.

"I love you, Quintus."

"And I, you, Vespasia."

Her soul warmed in joy as she sat in his hold and, when he cupped her chin and tilted her face up toward his, warmth spread and blanketed her body. His spirit seemed to envelope hers. He lowered his head and touched his lips to her. A tremor rippled through her.

Her senses became heightened by his slow, thoughtful kiss and the light breeze drifting by brought on another brief shiver. His kiss became more persuasive and, although she felt what they were doing should stop before their loving went further, she couldn't draw away. She met his command and parted her mouth, letting him taste her more fully. His teeth nicked her lips, his tongue caressed hers. When his hand moved from her chin to cup her head and his other arm stayed wrapped around her, she was grateful for his support. She imagined herself as a stream of free flowing liquid as he brought her desires and passion out.

Light, mobile, loose. That's how good she felt running beside Artim during the last stretch of the race. It seemed they connected on a metaphysical plane, and he fed his exuberant amount of energy to her. The last few miles went by in a blur and, when she saw the finish line and realized she had broken her goal of five hours by twenty minutes, she wanted to do cartwheels.

Close to the end, she grabbed his hand. They ran hand in hand through the gate. Volunteers placed finishers' medals around their necks and took the timing chips from their shoes. Once they were far enough down the chute to be out of peoples' ways, she threw her arms around him and gave him a huge kiss, square on his sexy lips.

A fling with Artim to get over Don was exactly the holiday gift she needed.

Chapter Three

"*Y*ou did what?"

Katie's voice shrilled behind Jenna. Jenna put her mascara down and looked at her friend's reflection in the mirror. Katie's short black hair with blonde, spiked tips didn't move a fraction as she shook her head and stared back.

"Is it so hard to believe that I have a date?" Jenna resumed her application of make-up.

"Uh, no, but *you* kissed a total stranger at the finish line and *you* asked him out."

"Yeah, boring, quiet, stoic little Jenna did something totally out of the ordinary. *She* picked up a guy and wants to celebrate with him." She blotted her lips with a tissue.

"Come on, Jenna, you know that's not what I meant."

"Yes, it was what you meant. I know you guys think I'm a stick in the mud." After a glance in the mirror appraising her overall appearance, she turned and propped herself against the counter. Katie appeared remorseful for her remark. "But that's okay. For the most part you're right. With teaching and research and my book, I haven't had much time for fun. But now all that's going to change."

"Good. You need to cut loose for once." Katie came up next to her, gazed into the mirror and tapped the tips of her spiked hair with the palm of her hand. "And you sure picked a winner from what you've already told me about him. But to kiss Artim so quickly after meeting him…that still doesn't sound too much like you."

"I know. Crazy, isn't it? The whole experience was strange. Running the marathon, meeting him, having weird images careen through my mind—"

"Weird images?"

"I kept picturing us as a couple in ancient Rome. We were presenting ourselves in public for our upcoming wedding."

Katie tisked. "You've had your nose in those historical books way too much. Now you're manifesting your research into reality." She spritzed her hair again.

Jenna waved her hand in front of her face to clear the air of the sticky spray. "I don't think those thoughts stemmed from my studies. After all, I really was trying to concentrate on the race. I don't know how to explain it, but I believe there's a connection between the two of us. It feels like I've known him forever. I was automatically comfortable with him and had the strongest desire to just stay with him, to be with him." She closed her eyes, remembering the softness of his hand on her arm when he'd kept her from falling on the course, the love emanating from the young version of him in her vision. With a sigh, she opened her eyes, glanced at the Jacuzzi tub to her right, then gazed out into the sleeping area at the king size bed. *If only I didn't have a roommate on this trip, Artim and I could enjoy the room's amenities.* There was always his room, she mused, but considering he was in the same hotel a few floors down and also had a roommate, there would be no privacy there, either.

"Oh Jenna, you're finally letting up on yourself and joining life's party. You don't know how happy this makes me." Katie put her hands over her heart and batted her eyelashes.

"Smart ass."

"Better than being a dumb one. So when do I get to see this Mr. Wonderful you've been gushing about?"

"In about half an hour." Jenna patted her on the back, then moved past her toward the bedroom. "Which doesn't leave you much time to get ready."

"Ready for what?" Katie balanced against one side of the double doorway.

Jenna dropped her robe and slipped into her favorite white blouse, which accentuated her curves, and a pair of tan slacks she'd laid out on the bed earlier. "To come with me."

"I'm not going with you." Katie pushed off the doorway and headed toward the other room of the suite where the couch and television were. "Two's company and three's a crowd."

The television clicked on. An announcer rattled off information about a local restaurant.

After Jenna put on a pair of comfortable flats, she joined her friend in the living area. "It won't be three. It'll be four. He has a friend who you're going to love."

"Really? And why is that?" She glanced over her shoulder, not looking too convinced.

"Because he's handsome and fit and he's a complete asshole. Just your type."

"Cool! I wondered what I would end up doing when you said you had a date." Katie bounded off the brown leather couch, hurried into the bedroom, threw open the closet doors and rummaged through her dresses. "So the little black dress?" her friend pulled out the garment and held it up. "Or the little red dress?" She displayed it next to the first outfit.

Jenna carefully assessed each one and decided she liked neither. Not that Katie's petite body wouldn't look hot in either one of them, but the hair spikes didn't do the dresses justice. And Jenna wanted her friend to be as sexy and attractive as possible. This way Ned would be focused on Katie and wouldn't bother her and Artim.

"What about your silver mini skirt with that purple and silver blouse and the black camisole halter top thing?"

"Great idea! And I can wear the purple pumps." She grabbed the items and went to the bathroom. "I'll be ready in time. No worries."

Katie shut the doors.

* * * *

"Just accept the fact you owe me, Ned, and move past it."

"I still can't believe you found her, Artim." Ned glared at him, his piercing gaze direct and probing. "Are you sure you didn't coerce her in any fashion? That she asked you out on her own freewill? You didn't touch her or anything like that?" Ned stomped onto the elevator and sulked in the opposite corner.

The doors met and securely shut. Artim gazed over at his longtime friend, not wanting to restart the argument they'd had, but Ned had to lose the scowl. "I don't want to fight." He let out a long sigh and closed his eyes. "So stop spewing the same questions at me, will you?"

"I'm not fighting. I'm just asking. What did you do? And even though I don't like the terms of the bet, why couldn't I have paid up before we went out?"

"It's like I told you before. I didn't do anything to sway the outcome one way or the other." Artim's voice rang loud and harsh in the small space. He took a deep breath, working to keep his temper in check. "I inadvertently touched her a couple of times. Once due to the crowd and another when I had to catch her before she planted her face in the asphalt. But I didn't force any thoughts or feelings on her. She also touched me once and then took my hand at the end. But again, I did nothing to influence the result of her kissing me or asking me out to celebrate. And I didn't want you to make good on the bet because I want to be completely sure it's her. Now, try to be happy and smile, damn it."

He turned from the scrutiny of Ned's glare. Even though Ned couldn't get into his mind and judge him on his actions and thoughts like he could with others, Artim still didn't like the way Ned's gaze bore into his, or the blatant, open way he tried to assess him to see if his thoughts met his approval or not.

So what if I gave her a couple jolts to her memory? Where was the harm in making someone's soul remember they loved you?

He had to have her back. The time apart from her had felt like an eternity. *Hell, since we had last been together had been an eternity.* Too much time had passed since he'd held her in his arms, tasted her sweetness, loved her through the night 'till the early hours of dawn. He needed her again like he needed to breathe. He couldn't continue one more day without her by his side.

Ned should be happy he'd found her. He'd told Ned enough times about their history and what had happened. His friend should have been more understanding that he would have made her remember who she was and who he was with any tactics he could. Granted, had he been the one to lose the bet his and Ned's mutual friend Dion had made them make before they left on the journey, he wouldn't have been thrilled either.

"She's not the same person you know."

Ned's statement and the holiday Muzak intruded upon Artim's thoughts. The truth of the matter sliced through him again and his jaw clenched. Both Dion and Ned had hammered that point home continuously from the moment he'd mentioned his quest of tracking her down. Of course she wouldn't be the demure senator's daughter who had begged him not to leave and who he'd left anyway. But a soul was a soul. He'd bet his position of power on that reasoning, and now that the current era had produced his love, he prayed his logic was correct and her soul hadn't changed.

"Stuff it, Ned. Don't you think I know that? You and Dion won't let me forget that she won't be the same woman." The doors to the elevator swished open. Artim stepped out with long purposeful strides. At the door to Jenna's room, he paused and looked at his friend. "Besides, if Tresa were around you'd be pissed, too, if your peers kept trying to stop you from being with her."

"True. But you and I both know where Tresa is and my chances of catching up to her are slim."

"But you do have the opportunity if you'd only pursue it."
He turned back to the door and knuckle-rapped on the wood.

* * * *

"You weren't kidding about Artim, Jenna," Katie drawled
quietly. "What a great catch for a rebound guy." She looked
over her shoulder, giving their dates another glance.

Jenna followed her gaze. The two men were several feet
back, mixing in with the crowd of tourists who had come to
see the holiday botanical gardens in the five star casino hotel.

"You weren't joking about Ned, either," she continued.
"I'm totally taken with his blue eyes. God, they're gorgeous,
but even for my weird tastes, he seems a bit standoffish and
too arrogant. Did you hear him at lunch mumbling how no
one seems to be deserving anymore? That people are too self-
centered? He talks about being self-centered, and he won't
even tell me his last name."

Artim caught Jenna staring at him so she whipped her
attention back to Katie. The flowers which created beautiful
displays of polar bears, candy canes, and holiday balls and the
decorated evergreen trees and reindeer whizzed by in a blur of
color. She patted her friend's arm and whispered, "You
should give him a chance. It could be that his race didn't go
the way he'd planned, and he's prickly about it."

Katie shrugged.

Artim walked up behind Jenna and placed a hand on the
curve of her lower back. Any fatigue she had melted away
with his gentle touch. All areas of her body roused with sparks
of passion. For the second time that day, her crotch
moistened and pulsated in need. The heat of embarrassment
rose and flamed in her cheeks. Fanning herself due to her
discomfiture would be too obvious, so she closed her eyes and
took a deep breath. While inhaling his rich spicy fragrance, an
image of the two of them facing each other and holding hands
while standing in front of a crowd flashed in her mind.

In the vision, she gazed into the eyes of her love and
quietly, lovingly spoke his name. "Quintus."

"What? Who's Quintus?" Katie's and Ned's voices rang in stereo on each side of her.

Artim chuckled and let go of Jenna's back. "As beautiful and breathtaking as the artistry of this flower garden is, might I suggest we head back to our room? We have a wonderful bottle of merlot we can open and drink. We can relax. Then, after evening falls, we can go…umm…how you say, paint the town red?"

"Sounds like a plan to me," Jenna and Katie chirped in unison.

Chapter Four

*J*enna stared at the backs of Artim's and Ned's heads in the van taxi on the way back to the hotel. Since her slip of tongue at the garden, the two men had bickered like an old married couple. Trouble was she couldn't understand what they were fighting about.

"Katie? You're the world traveler and linguist. Do you know what they're arguing over?" Jenna whispered.

"I wish I could figure out what their exact issue is, but Artim is ranting in a mix of Italian and another language I've never heard, and Ned's been responding in kind with a bit of German thrown in. All I've grasped so far is that there was a bet, Ned lost and Artim wants payment."

"Interesting." She stared out the window and admired the obelisks and palm trees in front of the black glass pyramid, trying to wrap her mind around how the men could fight over such a simple thing as a bet.

When the taxi stopped at the hotel, both men grew eerily quiet and continued the awkward silence as everyone made their way into the hotel, through the grand atrium and to the banks of elevators. Jenna admired a large, quartz crystal encased behind a glass panel in the wall and pretended to ignore the brooding men while waiting for an elevator.

Katie and Jenna stood behind the men in the elevator. If Jenna had a pin and dropped it, she'd have heard the thin piece of metal land on the plush carpet. She mouthed that she had no idea what was going on, and Katie shrugged a shoulder in response, apparently confused herself. The moment the doors swooshed open, Ned charged out and Artim stood to the side in gentlemanly fashion extending his arm for Katie and her to precede him.

In the men's suite, Ned headed straight for the bedroom while Artim opened the bottle of wine and poured a couple of glasses. "Ladies, make yourselves comfortable. I need to go have a word with Ned."

When he handed her the glass, his dark sensual gaze honed in on her eyes, his fingers brushed against hers and a thick beat of desire drummed through Jenna. She quickly drank the wine, hoping the glass would hide the blush enflaming her cheeks. The corners of his lips quirked in seeming amusement of her discomfort. He went into the bedroom and closed the door behind him. A few seconds later another set of doors slammed shut.

"The conversation must be serious if they've gone into the bathroom and closed those doors to talk." She sat on the couch and motioned to Katie to take a seat.

Katie shook her head. "I'm a little uncomfortable with how the men are acting." She drank the rest of her wine. "These new shoes are bugging me, too. I'm going to head back to our room and relax my feet. Let me know if there's going to be a second half to this date."

"No problem." Jenna clicked on the television after Katie left the room and flipped through the few available channels. Minutes passed and still no sign of the guys. While the infomercials of the hotel casino amenities were somewhat interesting, she soon grew bored. When the third replay of the steakhouse commercial came on, she rose from the couch and poured another glass of wine at the small wet bar. Jenna stared at the bedroom door and drank the red liquid, wondering what detained the men.

She tiptoed to the door and put her ear against it. No voices, muffled or otherwise, could be heard on the other side. A pang of concern rapped her senses so she carefully edged the door open to obtain a better bead on the situation. A moan from the bathroom cut through the silence and, imagining that one of the men had beaten the bloody pulp out of the other, she rushed to the doors and threw them open.

The sight before her made her take a step back, her jaw drop in surprise.

Ned hung limp in Artim's arms as Artim pressed his lips upon his forehead. Glowing purple outlined the area where Ned's skin met Artim's mouth.

Feeling like she intruded on a very intimate moment but couldn't escape, she cleared her throat.

Artim stopped kissing Ned's forehead and gently placed him down on the toilet. "This is not what it looks like, Jenna," Artim quickly offered.

She quirked an eyebrow. "Really? Because it sure looked like you were kissing him…or sucking out his brains."

"He was," Ned mumbled, shaking his head then running his fingers through his hair, appearing like a man rousing from a bender. The puckered circle of skin quickly lost it's magenta coloring and returned to normal. "I lost a bet and our friend Dion's idea of payment was for the winner to —"

"Ned!" Artim's voice boomed in the marbled area. "Jenna does not need to know about our arrangement." He turned his head, captured her gaze with his. "Do you, Jenna?"

His dark-eyed gaze flared with a warning and promised passion. Her blood boiled at the thought of being with him. Any questions or concerns about some stupid bet between them flittered from her mind. "Makes no difference to me one way or the other." She flipped a hand in the air as if to wave away whatever was going on in the room. "You didn't have to stop on my account." She so didn't want to be considered a prude by the two gorgeous men.

Ned stood on wobbly legs, appeared to have issues with his balance and orientating himself. "I'm going for a walk. I'll be back in a little while."

Artim nodded.

The man stumbled around her and shuffled out of the bathroom, mumbling about the loss of his powers for the next several hours.

Though she thought his rambles were strange, she was more concerned about his physical state. "You're just gonna let him go off alone? He doesn't seem to be in very good condition right now."

"Ned will be fine." Artim stepped forward and wrapped his arms around her. "How about we go sit on the couch and relax for a little bit with some wine and music?"

"Sounds lovely."

Moments later, she and Artim snuggled on the couch, sipping on their drinks and listening to jazz through the room's sound system. She found it amazing how they'd only met several hours ago but were already comfortable with silence between them.

"Feel free to nap," his deep, seductive voice rolled in her ear. He removed the glass from her hand.

Compelled to do as he said, she closed her eyes and drifted into a pleasant dream-like state.

Chapter Five

"**V**espasia? Come child. It's time to dress for your wedding."

Her mother's voice echoed through the family abode to her chamber. With sentimental wonder, she rose from her bed and took one last look around her childhood room. No longer would this be her quiet sanctuary where she could run to escape the world or sit in quiet contemplation. Soon she would be in a new home with a husband and, hopefully, children to care for. No longer would she have these moments of tranquil solitude.

A small sack containing her remaining belongings sat next to the doorway. The dowry promised to Quintus had been sent to their new home a few days prior and nothing of hers, save the bag, was left in the room.

One life ending and a new one beginning…

"Vespasia!"

"Coming mother!"

At the door she retrieved the receptacle and found her way to her mother's chamber.

"Put your bag on the stool over there, then come to me."

Vespasia did as her mother requested and, as she approached her, her mother held up the dress she had made from the white material she had discovered at the market. Although it had been worked and shaped by the elder's hands, the apparel was still pristine and pure.

"Undress yourself child."

After slipping out of her outfit, she allowed her mother to don her in her wedding dress. The robe, soft and comforting against her skin, was much longer and more enclosed than an everyday *peplos*. The bright light color of the cloth gave the illusion that her olive complexion deepened in color.

"Beautiful."

Nodding in agreement, she held her arms out to the sides as the elder woman wrapped her midsection with a gold hued rope belt and tied the length in front of her in the *Knot of Hercules*. As she turned to obtain the shoes and veil, Vespasia fingered the ends of the belt with a smile. To keep Hercules, the guardian of wedded life, pleased about the union, only her husband could undo the knot. *And once the belt is loosened and removed, he and I will be able to…* She shivered in anticipation.

"Sit, child, so I may place the bridal shoes on your feet."

Once comfortable and balanced on the stool her mother provided for her, the woman placed a dainty shoe, the color of the lemons hanging from the trees in the courtyard, on Vespasia's right foot, and then the other of the pair on her left. She wiggled my toes, which were used to the freedom of sandals, in the confines of the footwear.

"Try not to fidget too much today."

"I will do my best," Vespasia replied and bent her head toward the older woman to have the veil secured to her hair.

Completely clothed in her wedding ensemble, she stood and held hands with her mother.

"You make a lovely bride, my dear daughter, and you will make a fine wife."

Tears welled in the woman's eyes, so she released her hands and embraced her in her arms. Quietly she said, "Thank you, mother."

The next hour passed quickly as she waited in her mother's chambers. The clamoring of the wedding guests grew in the main part of the abode. Due to her father's status as a Senator and their many family members, they had more than enough witnesses to make their betrothal legal. It was nice they didn't have to worry about that aspect of the ceremony.

Before Vespasia knew it her bridesmaid entered the room and told her it was time. She and Secunda Sabina had been friends since they were toddlers. She had stood as bridesmaid for her last year, and Sabina was proud to return the favor for her this year. Sabina took her hand and led her from the room into the crowded front hall brimming with music and conversation.

Slowly the two strolled through the throng of guests. The more people congratulated her on the great match their families had made, the bigger her smile grew. Happiness consumed her and overflowed like a generously full cup of wine from the first barrel of the season at Quintus's uncle's vineyard. After having partaken a bit too much in his wonderful vintage before, she felt as giddy now as she had then. Everything she observed appeared crisp and clear. All their friends and family were resplendent dressed in their finery. The white walls and marble floors had been washed and were bright, reflecting the sun of the afternoon.

As Sabina continued to lead her into the courtyard where the priest waited, she caught the whispered positive appraisals regarding her intended and her mother's talent with the needle concerning her wedding outfit. The group of guests fell in line behind them to follow. The colors of the grass, the many flowers that lined the beds around the water features, and the water in the fountains shone in vivid detail in the courtyard that had been prepped for the ceremony. The setting could not have been more perfect, nor the day more beautiful. Again, she could not still the smile that enlivened her face as she nodded to the priest and Sabina took her position behind her.

A hush fell over the crowd. She turned her head. Quintus, handsome in his white and gold trimmed toga, edged his way through the throng of toga clad guests, sauntering toward her. Tears of joy welled in her eyes.

Standing before family and friends, Quintus and Vespasia grasped each other's hands. She gazed into his eyes and saw the love he felt for her. Sabina stood next to them, pulling a length of yellow cloth from the attachment on her belt.

Methodically and reverently, she wrapped their hands in the soft material which Vespasia would one day weave into other material for a blanket for their first child. Bound together, she and Quintus turned their attention to the priest.

The purple-robed older man with his wizened visage held up his arms. "May the place of this ceremony be sanctified by the gods," his voice boomed over the crowd, "for family and friends gather here in a ritual of love and devotion between two who would be joined for life and all eternity. Is it your desire and intention, Quintus, to become one with Vespasia?"

"*Sic. Quando tu Gaius, ego Gaia.*"

When he gazed upon her with love in his eyes and a smile upon his lips, and stated his longing to be with her, a joyous tear streamed down her cheek.

"Is it your desire and intention, Vespasia, to become one with Quintus?"

I am blessed to have such a good match with someone I love and whom I do not mind spending eternity with.

"*Sic. Quando tu Gaius, ego Gaia,*" her voice rang loud and clear so all guests could hear her acceptance of the man she loved. To Quintus she quietly repeated, "Yes. When and where you are Gaius, I then and there am Gaia."

From the side Sabina brought two stools for them to sit on and removed the cloth from their hands. Quintus and Vespasia faced the altar as the priest blessed them with more words and prepared the oblation to Jupiter.

The man faced us again and held up a large piece of cake on a white cloth. "Jupiter, with this offering, I request unto you to be kind and indulgent to this couple who have bonded in love this day, to the children they will have, and to the household they will create together. Oh, great Jupiter, you are worshiped with this offering." After he lowered the cake, he broke it in two and handed each of them a piece, which they ate in solemn silence.

Jupiter was then honored with wine, and once they had drunk the liquid, a cheer rang from the crowd.

Hand in hand, Quintus and Vespasia made their way to the banquet table.

The dinner with its many courses, lively banter and festive music rushed by in a blur and, before she knew it, three of her young male cousins, one of them with a torch, approached them. Vespasia, knowing this was all part of the ceremony, let two of them pull her from the table and support her by the arms. The procession was necessary for the completion of the betrothal.

The boys led her from the table and they headed the assemblage to the house Quintus had built not far from his uncle's home on a hill above the vineyard. Many of the townspeople joined in the parade for fun. Vespasia believed they joined the gathering for the sheer enjoyment of being able to mix with the guests and pellet members of the Senate with nuts, knowing they couldn't be punished for abusing their betters during the wedding custom.

Once on top of the hill overlooking the yard where grapes grew, Vespasia's mother held her in her arms outside the door to the house built for her husband and her. Quintus, with a pretend show of force, pulled her from her arms.

The cousin with the torch handed it over to Vespasia's mother who handed it to her. Several feet from her new home was an outdoor pit and, as she strolled over to the place for the ceremonial fire, she chanted, *"Quando tu Gaius, ego Gaia."* She lit the wood in the pit, extinguished the light of the torch and tossed the burnt stick into the crowd.

"You are all free to stay and celebrate," Quintus called out to the revelers. "Food and drink, provided by my generous uncle, can be found over there." He pointed to tables set to the left of the fire pit. "Vespasia and I thank you for coming." With his last words, he swept Vespasia up into his arms and carried her over the threshold of their home, kicking the door shut behind them.

* * * *

"Happy Saturnalia, Vespasia, my love." Quintus walked into the bedroom and took her in his arms.

Vespasia returned his hug, placing her head against his shoulder. "Happy Saturnalia, my love. Can you believe we've been wedded for six months?"

"Time has passed quickly, but with each day my love for you has grown."

"As mine has for you," she replied and gazed at him.

Before she could take her next breath, his mouth descended on hers. His hands slid up her back, clasped her shoulder and brought her chest closer to his. His mouth sensuously moved upon hers and, when it parted, she followed suit.

The heat generated between them was intense, and she believed she would melt into nothingness. It had been that way on their wedding night when he claimed her for the first time, and the sensations repeated each time they'd come together since. And as always, she couldn't seem to get near enough to her love, her husband. Her fingers splayed across his shoulders and trailed a path up the side of his neck to cup his face in her hands. She forced his mouth open farther with her tongue, pulled his into hers, sucked on it, and gave it a playful nip before she let it go.

Her lips savored the feel of his, the way they caressed, the way they glided smoothly against hers. Again in perfect accord, they deepened the kiss. His embrace fit her snugly to him. She was aware of each place his body touched hers and contentment eased her muscles. His lips pulled from hers again, only a feather's touch did they remain connected, and she sighed happily.

He carried her to their large, luxurious, white sheet and pillow covered bed. When he lay upon the piece of furniture with her buttocks on his lap, the extent of his arousal pressed upon her. With a passionate advance, she claimed his lips with her own and again slipped her tongue into his mouth, tasting

the dark berries, oak and spice of the wine he had drunk with
dinner.

His tongue searched her mouth. Primitive hunger swelled
and took over. Matching his movements with a natural flare
that they had developed in the few months of their marriage,
she ran her fingers through his soft hair, reveling in its
silkiness.

She shifted on his lap, then rose. As she disrobed, he
followed suit and their naked bodies came together when she
took her place on his lap again. With her gaze trained on his,
she positioned her hands on his shoulders. Methodically, she
slid them down, feeling all the contours and nuances of his
upper torso. He sucked in his breath when her fingers
brushed over his nipples, the skin of his chest beneath her
fingers hairless, soft, and so hot. She continued to smooth a
path down to his abdomen. The outlines of muscles tensed,
shuddered, released, and at the boundary of his triangle, she
stopped and then retraced her way back up his trunk. With
her thumbs, she brushed his nipples again and he quivered.
She lovingly caressed his breasts once more.

She rubbed an outward trail to his sides and skimmed
downwards. He was so sturdy and warm. The subtle scent of
his manly musk, earth and grapes intoxicated her senses. She
ran her tongue down the valley of his chest.

Spreading her palm against his navel, she rotated her hand
and extended her fingers. When they hit their mark, she
grasped his hard shaft, tugged and licked its head. His hips
thrust towards her and with that invitation she took him in
her mouth. He was silky smooth and, as he grunted and
stirred under her head, she continued her mouth massage,
savoring him. Moisture flooded between her legs as she
pleasured the man beneath her. She then realized she wanted
him inside her, touching her soul.

Vespasia glanced up at her love, her nipples immediately
peaking and hardening in the cool air. He shuddered and his
hooded, passion-filled gaze met hers. She smiled slyly and,

with her gaze still connected to his, gave the tip of his cock a quick flick of her tongue. He threw his head back. A heated groan escaped from his lips. She stroked his penis with her hand from its base to its tip, tightening her grip ever so slightly on the up-slide.

Lightly tracing the backs of her fingers along the bottom of his abdomen, she trailed them down along his hips and thighs, then smoothed her hands back up his legs and into their juncture to cup his balls. She placed his cock back in her mouth and moaned, sending a delightful vibration along his shaft. Her head bobbed up and down rhythmically, enticing him to greater heights.

When she thought he couldn't take anymore, she spread her form on top of him, her breasts pressing down on his, her crotch hairs teasing his cock. His massive, firm body didn't budge or twitch. *Such a solid, strong man.*

A moment later he had her on her back and moved down her length. Vespasia gazed upon the man who knelt between her thighs and watched as he made himself comfortable near her crotch.

The touch of his tongue within the fissure of her labia sent her mind whirring with ecstasy. And the kiss of his lips on her clit made her hips buck toward the ceiling of their abode. As he lapped and suckled her pussy, she grabbed his hair, entwining her fingers in the long shaggy cuts.

A few times he casually kissed her along the length of her crotch, but that never lasted long for his tongue and fingers would continue their explorations. She moaned and writhed under his arousing assault, her juices flowing and adding to the experience. She clutched the bed sheets.

Slowly he climbed up, positioned himself and entered her. His mouth latched on to her right nipple and as he teased the peak with his tongue, tingles of pleasure trickled up and down her body. She shifted to give him more access to her breast and a delightful sensation stirred in her muscles around his cock. Vespasia circled her hips slightly.

As he continued to suckle one breast and caress the other, her hips rose to meet him in desperate yearning for release and, as he delved in deeper, she believed he hit her center, her soul. The love she felt for him engulfed her whole being. Several times he repeated the action and each movement increased the fire burning within her, until finally she dug her nails into his back and let herself fall into the abyss of sexual pleasure. Joining and separating in a heated frenzy, sweat slicked them as they panted and gasped in escalating bliss. They exclaimed almost in unison when their closely timed orgasms racked their bodies. After the waves of desire crashing through her body calmed, a knock at the front door prompted him to climb off, dress and leave the room.

Vespasia followed, wrapping a sheet around herself as she left the room and quietly padded down the hall. Right outside the front door, Quintus chatted with a man she'd never seen before. Upon overhearing the stranger say *Mithras*, her blood ran cold and she shrunk back into the shadows to listen to the rest of their conversation.

When Quintus shut the door and turned back into the house, she stepped from her hiding spot, stood in front of him and looked up into his beautiful eyes.

Vespasia dropped to the floor, wrapping her arms around his lower legs, hugging them tightly. She let her tears and fears loose as she pleaded with him, "I sense danger in this meeting you plan to attend. Please, Quintus, do not leave me."

Chapter Six

*J*enna rolled over in the bed fitfully, stirring from the dream and her sleep, when a woman's voice drifted to her ears. A few beats later, laughter rang from the other room and she realized the voice was Katie's.

She sat up on the bed and scratched her head, a little disorientated and wondering how she'd ended up back in her room. The curtains were open. Outside the sky blanketed the city in inky darkness. She rose, stretched, and went over to the hotel room window. Down below, thousands of lights sparkled and twinkled from the many housing and shopping developments built on the desert floor. Looking out upon the pretty, golden view, which extended for miles, a contented glow spread through her after having such a long interesting day.

But why am I here and not waking in Artim's arms?

"Oh good, you're up." Katie walked in and closed the flap of her cell phone.

"How did I get here? How long have I been here? Where's Artim?" The questions shot out in a subconscious frenzy, as panic over Artim's absence hit her.

"Artim carried you up about an hour ago. You were out cold. I guess if you had to be carted to a room by a guy and do so unnoticed, Vegas is the place to do it. No one thinks twice about what goes on around here, do they?"

She shot Katie an impatient scowl.

"Sorry. I digressed a bit, didn't I?" Katie shook her head and held out a piece of paper. "Where he is, I'm not sure.

Maybe the note he scribbled in his haste to get out of here will tell you."

Jenna took the paper, stared at it, then glared at her friend. Katie's voice and expression had oozed with pity. The vein beside Jenna's right eyebrow pulsed in a slow, thick rhythm as her jaw clenched. Yet she had no cause to be angry with Katie. Artim's dump-and-run wasn't her fault. But she still wanted to smack the troubled look off her face and the thought *poor little Jenna lost another guy* out of her mind, which she knew was rambling around in her friend's brain.

Her breath hitched as she looked back down at the folded note, her heart aching and thumping in achingly slow tempo. Her stomach rolled. Clutching the note in her fist, she hurried to the bathroom where the bright lights would give her ample opportunity to read his words.

My dearest Jenna:

Oh dear God, it is a Dear John *letter.* Tears welled in her eyes blurring the letters on the page. Behind her Katie answered her cell phone and she watched in the mirror as Katie vacated the bedroom. She blinked so she could make out the words on the page.

I am truly sorry to have to leave so soon. Ned and I got called back to duty due to an emergency. I don't know if I will be able to come back…in time…to return to you. If I thought you could accept me for who I really am, I'd have fought to have you come with me. But I don't want to impose my lifestyle upon you, have you give up your life. Know that you will be forever close to my heart. Artim de Sutcivnilos

P.S. Tell Katie Ned's full name is Ned Odognagap.

The note dropped from Jenna's hand as she clutched the edge of the bathroom counter.

Why couldn't he have given me a chance to choose? Why did he just leave me here?

The well of tears broke and escaped her eyes. Salty water streamed down her cheeks, currents finding their way on and in between her lips. As she took in a shuddering breath, her gaze landed on the reflection of the note in the mirror. She wiped the wet from her eyes and face with a bath towel, then looked more closely at the mirror image. Amazed, she grabbed the paper and held it up to the mirror to make sure she read Artim's name correctly.

Artim de Sutcivnilos translated in the reflection as *solinvictuS ed mitrA.*

Mithras, her dream-self whispered in shock.

Jenna's mind, full of her studies, research and lectures rattled off information. Mitra, or Mithras, was the principal figure of the Greco-Roman religion of Mithraism. Vedic Mitra was the patron divinity of honesty, friendship, contracts and meetings. Sol Invictus was a religious title applied to at least three distinct divinities during the later Roman Empire of which Mithras, or Mitra as he was also called, was one. Deus Sol Invictus, the unconquered sun god, was a god of the late Roman state, worshiped by a cult created by Elagabalus, which continued until paganism was abolished.

The images. The dreams.

I am *Vespasia.*

Sitting on the edge of the tub, she clutched the paper to her breast bone and squeezed her eyes shut. The dream she'd had earlier picked up where it had left off.

"Please, Quintus, do not go to the woods tonight. I do not want you participating in the ceremony. I have heard men have died during the rites."

"Do not fear." He lovingly brushed a hand against her cheek. *"No harm will come to me and no matter what happens I will always be with you and close to your heart."*

After opening her eyes and smoothing out the crinkled paper, Jenna reread the words at the bottom. *Know that you will be forever close to my heart.*

He's left me. Again.

The paper slipped from her grasp and floated to the floor. She placed her face in her hands so she could weep, but the images from her distant past wouldn't let her be.

A forest scene played on her mind's screen, the place to where she as Vespasia had covertly followed Quintus.

Vespasia had told him she would follow. And shadow him she did into the dark, thick woods outside of town, disregarding his warnings about what would happen should she be caught by the men in the group. Her safety and being found out wasn't what concerned her. What worried her was the risk her husband had decided to take by attending his cult meeting at the beginning of Saturnalia.

Hiding behind a few trees and a thicket of bushes, she watched the black cloaked men circle in heavy, exaggerated walking steps around a large stone table. Drums quietly thumped out a slow, eerie beat, to which the assembled chanted, and shadows, created from the bright flames of the surrounding fire pits, danced on the backs of the cloaked ones. Many long minutes passed. The men moved, intoning their foreign words, until a booming voice ordered them to stop.

Next to the stone table the men roughly handled Quintus and disrobed him. He struggled against his co-members, shouting he wasn't the chosen one.

The leader, she assumed since he was the only one clad in a red robe, stepped into the group. "The great one has changed his mind. He has decided you, Quintus, would be his subject, his eternal host." The man's voice carried over the distance to her.

Her skin crawled with his statements.

The men placed Quintus on the table and tied his wrists and ankles. Her love let loose an unearthly scream and her blood froze. A man forced a gag into his mouth to cut off his piercing wails. He fought against the restraints, bashing his body against the gray stone slab. The chanting intensified and the red-robed one raised his hands to the sky, speaking a litany to his god.

Vespasia wanted to rush to Quintus's side and help him, but she knew that wouldn't be a smart move. She stuck her tongue between her teeth and clamped down to keep herself from crying out.

Moments later a bright column of gold light beamed down from the heavens and penetrated the center of Quintus's body. His torso bent upward from the table and another scream roared from him.

The men cheered and resumed their chanting and dancing. The red-robed man waved his arms above Quintus and continued to invoke the spirit. Quintus thrashed upon the table, his muffled screams dwindling to stifled horrified groans.

She ran from the woods as if Cerberus nipped at her heels. She couldn't bear to see her love die.

The damn cult.

In the home she and Quintus shared, she threw herself upon the bed and cried herself to sleep.

Her love was gone, killed for the sake of the members having a few minutes with a god.

The next day a man whom she recognized from the night before showed up on her doorstep. He delivered the news about Quintus, which of course she already knew, but she feigned surprise anyway.

"He is no longer of this earth," he said, then turned and walked away.

Jenna's eyes flew open. She stood up from my place on the tub and retrieved the paper from the floor.

Her mind chewed over what the man had said in her dream. *No longer of this earth.* Not *he's dead.*

She held the note toward the mirror to view his name again and take closer note of Ned's. Mithras. Mitra. Artim. She gasped. That ancient god was the one who possessed him, but Quintus was still a viable participant in the body's existence, taking on a different name to appease his *guest*.

Ned, she realized, was the pagan god Oden. Lovely, she thought. He was the god the people in Germany believed made night-time flights through the sky during the holidays in mid-winter. The people feared him since he supposedly scrutinized the folk, deciding who deserved to prosper or perish. Because of his watchful presence, many people preferred to stay at home.

No wonder he was such a pill during the race and made such bizarre comments at lunch.

Jenna scurried from the bathroom and headed toward the main door.

"Where are you going?"

"I need to try and catch Artim."

"Dressed like that?"

She looked down at the hotel robe wrapped around her and wondered when she'd put it on. "I don't care. I have to find him."

Katie called out to her as she rushed from the room and down the hall to the elevator, but she didn't catch what she'd said. At the moment, she didn't care either. All she could focus on was finding Artim.

In the lobby, she frantically searched for him. Jenna ran to the middle of the grand foyer, spun to search the area, then stopped and stared out the doors several yards in front of her.

People passed by looking at her like she was crazy. *I am crazy.* She was in a classy hotel foyer dressed in slippers and a robe and in love with a god. She probably looked like she had just woken up. Jenna threaded her fingers through her hair and grasped it as tears streamed down her cheeks.

At the information podium, she inquired with the clerk if she had seen a man fitting the description she gave. The young lady shook her head. Jenna looked toward the reception area and desk momentarily thinking the representatives there could help, then remembered Katie said he had dropped her off in the room an hour ago.

He was gone, really and truly vanished from her life.

Jenna turned from the entrance way and shuffled toward the elevators, her heart broken, feeling lonelier than she ever had in her present and past lives.

"Jenna!"

She spun toward the lobby and saw Artim standing in the middle of it. Not caring for propriety, she ran to him and jumped in his arms. "Why did you leave me?" she sobbed into his shoulder.

"Because this time I thought it was the right thing to do. I knew what you were dreaming about, knew where it would lead and figured if you learned what had happened all that time ago you would hate me. But I can't give you up. Not again."

She pulled away slightly, her gaze peering into his. Images of whitewashed buildings with grand columns and rolling fields of grape vines and impressions of better and easier times filled her mind. Her soul warmed. She sighed in his embrace, enjoying the sensation of coming home to rest after a harrowing journey. Her lips pressed upon his and within moments her tongue entwined with his, exploring his mouth, gliding along his teeth, his lips and back. She reveled in the taste of him, tried to get closer to him, wanting to get inside him, partake of his power and strength…become one with him. Jenna delighted in how he returned her kiss with his own zeal and she sank deeper into him, exerting one last deep kiss of her own.

Withdrawing and resting her forehead against his, she caught her breath. "I'm so happy you came back. To think, if only you hadn't left the first time." She laid her head upon his shoulder.

"Yes, well, the first time I was blinded by delusions of grandeur with the cult and thought it would elevate me in my public standing. I was stupid. You were right that day when you sensed danger. I'm so sorry I went to the meeting. I had no idea what the Grand Master had planned. Luckily though, when Mitra had taken over my body and given me immortality and power he couldn't take over my spirit. That's why we remember each other. The reincarnated spirit of Vespasia within you recognizes my spirit. I've been waiting and searching for you for ages, and finally fate's brought us together. I love you, always have, always will."

Happy tears spilled from Jenna's eyes at his declaration. He wiped them away with his thumbs.

"I want you to join me," he stated. "Could you be a forgotten god's partner forever? Marry me here in Vegas. We can celebrate this festive season and our eternity together in style. Whatever your heart desires will be yours."

She threw her arms over his shoulders and planted another long, leisurely kiss on him. After it slowly ended, she kissed his cheek and whispered in his ear, "I would be happy to be your love for eternity. When and where you are my holiday spirit, I then and there am."

Yes, marrying her Quintus, her Artim, her soul mate, was exactly the holiday gift she needed.

Change of Fate

Chapter One

Just one touch and it will all be over.

Tresa recalled information on the job missive she'd received earlier as she stepped into a bedroom.

Henry O'Neil. Eighty-two. Married to childhood sweetheart, Emily. Together for sixty-two years. History of heart disease and diabetes. Slated for quietus at two-thirty-two in the morning.

She studied the sleeping couple. Their slow, rhythmic breaths moved their chests up and down in unison. *Sixty-two years.* She shook her head, unable to imagine being with someone for that long, having been robbed of the chance to. Fate had pretty much made sure she'd never be with her love again and experience years upon years of togetherness with him. Affection, family and home had been torn from her a long time ago, along with her humanity. It was true she had the opportunity to experience an eternal love with the deity who transformed her, but to his utter dismay, the fact that he had saved her life, desired her, didn't concern her. No matter how much he had claimed he yearned for her, she couldn't return the sentiment. She had made it clear she didn't want him and for that he had sentenced her to a lone existence across the ocean far from her home. She seethed with mounting rage at the injustice of her life being taken too soon.

Tresa clutched the scythe, the tool of her trade, in both hands, repelling the urge to release her frustration and attack the room. Its curved single-edged blade would nicely hack and slice everything to shreds.

The staff heated in her clenched fist. Taking that as a sign her task was about to begin, she removed the hood of her black cloak from her head and neared the antique four-poster bed.

Henry stirred, his breath hitched. A raspy expulsion of air and gurgling in his lungs followed.

Tresa reached deep down into her psyche, tried to draw up a smidgen of pity for what was about to occur, but nothing happened. She sighed. What did she expect? Her capacity to be sympathetic and compassionate had been stripped from her as well when she had crossed to the other side and been forced to take the psychopomp position of Grim Reaper. She was without heart now, a spirit destined to take the souls of others. With each assignment, she hoped to receive her soul back, or be released from her position and reincarnated into a new life, but she had a feeling neither would ever happen.

Emily stirred, muttered unintelligible words and nudged her husband while rolling over on the small mattress. Henry gasped and bolted upright. The white bed sheet fell away. He clutched his bare, frail chest at the base of his throat, appeared to fight for air. The man's round face morphed from a healthy pink to deep crimson with shades of violet. His gaze jerked around the room, then landed on Tresa, widening in recognition of who and what she represented.

"No. I'm not ready yet," he panted, dragging his other arm up and out, a motion to shoo her away.

"Henry?" Emily woke, sat up and shook her husband's arm. Her cloudy-eyed gaze searched the room. "What is it? What are you looking at?"

With strained effort, Henry lifted his arm, pointed the shaking extremity and a finger in Tresa's direction. "That, Emily. I'm looking at that." The words sputtered in a spray of pale red spittle.

"But I don't see anything." Her gaze glanced around the room once more before settling on her husband. A startled cry escaped her. "Henry, your mouth, it's covered in blood."

He swiped his lips with the back of his hand and stared in horror at the dark color on his pale skin. "Emily, get me my meds."

The woman scrambled from the bed and grabbed the phone in a blur of light blue nightgown as she hurried to the bathroom a few steps away. Her terrified voice on the phone with emergency services and movement of pill containers sounded from the small room.

Tresa glided to the side of the bed. The wrinkled-skin man gazed at her with a mixture of wonder and fright, his blanched brown eyes watered, his lips trembled. Not one part of Tresa twitched under the man's scrutiny. He could look all he wanted for all she cared since in a matter of moments he wouldn't remember a thing. Plus, she had given up wondering what her charges thought of her, what they saw when she stood before them. No doubt she was a ruthless sight to behold with her implacable countenance, bone white skin, auburn hair and forest green eyes. At least that's what she remembered her hair and eyes to look like. She wasn't sure if they still held the same color or not because she no longer reflected in mirrors. But she no longer cared about her lost looks or feelings. After all, she was a heartless bitch.

Henry gasped for air again, gazed down at his hands and kept his head bowed. "This is it, isn't it?" He peeked up at her.

She tilted her head in acknowledgement. The small motion was all she could do. The Grim Reaper couldn't offer a comforting smile, couldn't stroke his balding head covered in age spots and tufts of fine white hair, couldn't hold him and tell him it would be all right. If she touched a human, he or she would die.

"I'm coming, Henry. Hold on," Emily called from the bathroom. "Ah, found them."

The blade of Tresa's scythe lit in a ghostly fiery blaze. The time had come. She reached out to the wheezing man. The white of her long thin arm and hand glowed in the silver sheen of moonlight streaming in through the window, appeared like bones. The tip of her index finger touched and rested for a moment on Henry's forehead. Through the contact, she extracted his soul, pictured the essence traveling on a path to another plane and sent it on its way. She removed her finger and drew away from him to stand near the wall.

Henry clutched the left side of his chest. His eyes rolled into his head, became milky white orbs in an ashen face. The last breath he took expelled in a slow, shaky exhale. He fell back onto the bed. The fluffy pillows and thick comforter silenced the old man's body with a muffled thump.

Emily scuttled from the bathroom, open medication container in hand, and stopped short upon seeing her prostrate husband. The pill separator hit the floor and its contents tapped and rolled their way on the hardwood in several directions. Emily grabbed the sides of her face and wailed. "Henry, dear God, Henry!" She stumbled to the bed and shook him, then stuck the edge of her fist in her mouth when she failed to rouse him. Tears coursed down her face.

Downstairs, the doorbell rang. Emily released her hand, glanced around as if not recognizing the sound, then somberly rose from the bed and left the room. Her gut wrenching sobs filled the house.

The flames surrounding Tresa's blade disappeared. She took one last look at the man on the bed, raised her hood and, with a thought, dematerialized.

She reappeared on the rooftop of a bank at the top of a tall hill and sat on the edge of the edifice, dangling and swinging her legs back and forth over the side. Tresa gazed at the surroundings and enjoyed the quiet moments of her favorite time of year—fall and the thinning of the veil. Hours since she completed her job had ticked by and golden rays of sun lingered over autumn colored trees lining a river, illuminated the shopping complex and nearby houses. Traffic whizzed by on the highway. Soft daylight lit the grocery store and smaller retail outlets around the bank.

Tresa shook her head at the sight of the plaza and the people scurrying about. There once was a time when the hill had no buildings, no huge mass of population littering the area. Forest and pastures had dominated the region. The natural environment had given sanctuary to all types of creatures and humans who loved the land. This place had once reminded her of home and helped to alleviate her frustration. But to her dismay, those days, filled with the beautiful characteristics of nature that soothed her anger, were long gone.

Countless decades had passed and her love's betrayal and accusations still stung and boiled her blood. Because of one man's damning allegations, she had become a figment of people's dark imaginations and fears, a shadow lingering in one's peripheral vision, a cold chill raising the hair on their skin. She hung head and tamped down the raging tides of resentment within her. The hood hid her face, not that the concealment mattered. No one but the dying ever saw her.

The hood and sleeves of the cloak lifted from a breeze, floated off her body for a few seconds before settling into place again. She readjusted the clothing and re-secured the ties to ward off another gust of cool air.

Cool air? A breeze? Astonished by the physical sensations, the thoughts froze in her mind and her spine straightened. Nothing on the corporeal plane affected her. Ever.

Another current of air brushed over her, bringing with it a whiff of a spicy and sweet scent. The familiar aroma knocked on locked doors to her memory, but the lack of recall wasn't of concern. The fact she smelled and felt the air again was. For ages, the only emotions she had left were her frustrations and anger over being swindled of life and love. The only senses that had remained were her hearing and touch when it came to her clients and scythe. Never through the years during the time when the veil thinned between worlds was she able to sense anything not in relation to her job.

Tresa stood on the roof, surveyed the surroundings once more. The bright light hampered her vision. Water trickled from the corners of her eyes. She blinked and wiped the wet away. The tree's colors deepened. Their vividness stole her breath for a second.

What makes this year different from all the others?

The fragrance came again, sharper, stronger. She breathed deep, took in the air, picked apart the pleasant odor. Apples. Rich spices. A hint of sweet. *Apple cider.* She smiled. The smells evoked recollections of happier days gone by and of Jurgen Elman, the love of her human life so long ago in Germany—the man who made her heart sing, who showed her how great intimacy and passion could be, how wonderful living was. They both loved the warm drink and autumn with its crisp air, the colors, the festivities of Samhain.

Tresa jumped off the building and flew through the air, skimming the treetops and following the river, determined to find where the scent originated. She wasn't sure why she had her senses back, but she did know one thing for certain. If she ever came across Jurgen's soul, the bastard who condemned her to a friendless, loveless, eternity, she'd exact her revenge without qualms, long lost love or not.

Chapter Two

*T*resa followed the scent to its conclusion, landing next to a grand oak tree on the property of a Protestant church. Two women, dwarfed by rounded Doric columns and massive doors and windows, stood on the front steps of the white building. Up the long sloped sidewalk from them and next to the attached ancillary building, two men, both tall and with lean muscular physique, chatted in the parking lot, their backs to her. She scanned the people and the section of graveyard visible behind the church then looked to her scythe. No blue symbols or other signs for an upcoming job presented themselves. Confused, she cocked her head and zoned in on the conversations, hoping they'd reveal the reason why she was led to the place and them.

"All I know is that Jenna's a bit put off by your attitude the past couple of nights. She thinks you're acting weird." The dark-haired man turned, his Romanesque features softened by a smile, and waved at the women. They waved back. The one with brown hair and an athletic build blew a kiss. Her petite companion tilted a head covered with black hair and blonde spiked tips and clasped her hands together in front of her chest. A sappy look adorned her face.

"Me? Acting weird?" The second man threw his head back and laughed.

The blonde's good-natured mirth caught Tresa off guard, reminding her of another's laughter. The scenery's intensity wavered. Colors dimmed for a few seconds then returned to their original brilliance. The green grass of the graveyard, the black of the pavement, and white church contrasted against the blue sky. She searched her mind for a face to put with the remembered joy, but the recollection faded before she could retrieve it.

"Yes, you, Ned. You've seemed skittish and preoccupied. What's up?"

"I don't know, Artim." Ned shook his head and shoved his hands into the pockets of his jeans. "This time I'm stumped. Maybe it's the fall air and countryside stirring memories in me I'd rather keep buried. Maybe it's that I have this need to hone in on someone and judge them, but I'm blocked. I try to access people's thoughts and can't. It's strange not being able to do my job, something that's come second nature to me for centuries." He chuckled. "Maybe it's due to you winning the bet last December and taking over my duties for twenty-four hours. I don't think I've been quite right since. Or maybe right now it's all due to that awesome apple cider we had to drink at the mill the other night. I can't get it out of my mind."

"Can't get what out of your mind, babe?" The dainty black-haired woman in a pair of high-heeled shoes and too short, hot-pink, form-fitting dress clicked up to him.

"Those apples and the cider." Ned turned and hugged her, staring in the direction of the tree over her shoulder.

Tresa gasped. *Can the human see me?* She bent down to the ground. His gaze didn't follow. She stood and focused on his eyes. Over the years, she had learned eyes were the mirrors to one's soul. Many times in the course of her profession she had gazed into the dying's eyes and had seen the person's inner light or darkness, a technique she had developed to confirm the soul's destination. She had never attempted the trick on a living being but figured now was a good time to try it.

Taking a deep breath and focusing harder, she pried into the man's mind. *He's a strong one, knows how to block his thoughts.* She pushed past the barriers, observing his reactions as she went. He furrowed his brow, released the woman and straightened. *He's an old soul and senses my presence. He's known many people, been many places, lived many lives.* Tresa paused in her assessment and chewed on her bottom lip. *That doesn't seem right.* She quirked an eyebrow and rescanned him. *Lived one life. The life he's in right now. Another immortal is on the earth!* Enthralled about the knowledge, she pulled out of his essence to ponder the news and leaned against the tree.

Perhaps his presence is what sparked the changes I've noticed. She propped her scythe against the tree, crossed her arms over her stomach and smiled. *Someone like me, an enduring entity, has appeared. Someone I can talk to, other than the dying.* But was communication with a being like him, who lived in the physical world, possible? Would she want to know him? Men, after all, weren't high on her list of likes.

Once more, she squinted her eyes, trained her gaze on the blonde-haired man with striking Germanic features and extracted information. She searched his soul trying to determine what he was, *who* he was, and discovered the answer she sought. He was Oden, the pagan God people in Germany believed made nighttime flights through the sky during the holidays in midwinter. The folk feared him due to his scrutiny and decisions on who should prosper and who should perish. She delved deeper into his psyche and a profound sense of love and loss swept through her. He had caused great heartache. He bore unfathomable pain in regard to a past judgment concerning theft and betrayal. A long-ago pronouncement made against a woman, one he claimed to love. She examined the memory and unburied the woman's name. Tresa Grauenvoll.

Scheiße! Of all the names in creation, it was hers she unearthed from the dark recesses of his mind. She concentrated on him again, pictured his hair longer with thick waves, imagined him dressed in different clothes, and the man she had loved so long ago came into view. Recollections about the day Jurgen pointed his finger at her, named her as the one who committed the crime, ignited her temper. She jolted off the tree and grabbed her scythe, white knuckling the staff. *He thinks about my betrayal!* Zum Teufel! *So much for having someone else to talk to, to hang out with.* Old fury gushed through her like a geyser. This time she didn't hold her outrage at bay. She stormed up the small hill toward the group of people, the long handle of her tool clutched in both hands ready to strike. The folds of her cloak swished in furious rhythm against her bare legs. Dark clouds gathered over head. Thunder roared in the distance.

Verdammen Sie zu Hölle, Jurgen, she shouted, feral rage focused between her mind and his, believing with all her might the message would make it across the spiritual divide. *Kann Gott Spucke auf der Hure Sie sind mit und Sie.*

Ned released the woman from his arms and stepped back. A confused expression contorted his face. "Did you hear that? Someone just told me to go to hell, and that God should spit on me and the whore."

Artim snickered and covered his mouth. The brunette's jaw dropped.

"Who you calling a whore?" The spiked-hair woman shoved Ned's shoulder.

"It wasn't me, Katie." Ned held up his hands in front of him, palms facing her. "I tell you it was a voice I heard."

Katie huffed and turned her back on him, her arms crossed in front of her.

"Great. Now he's hearing voices." Jenna waved an arm in Ned's direction. "Didn't I say he's been acting weird, Artim?"

Unconcerned about the others, Tresa focused on the blonde-haired man and positioned the scythe in preparation to swing. Her intent was to decapitate Ned, the bastard she once knew as Jurgen, but she didn't expect it to happen. The blade couldn't hurt a body on the physical plane since it existed on a spiritual one. Still, her hope was her assault would do some kind of damage. She shifted her hands and caught the man's attention.

His blue-eyed gaze widened in surprise. His skin paled to match the church several yards away. *Tresa?*

Her name whispered in her mind, a soft caress she hadn't experienced since she had been transformed into the Grim Reaper. For a brief moment she considered dropping her weapon but didn't. She had waited lifetimes to inflict her revenge, to repay him for the hurt he had caused her. She smirked. *Hello, Jurgen.* The blade swung down and sliced through his neck.

Chapter Three

*N*ed grabbed his neck and crashed to his knees on the pavement. Pain shot up his thighs, reverberated through his bones. He screamed, but no sound came out of his gaping mouth. His breath hitched in his chest. Air didn't want to pass in or out of his throat. The world spun around him like he was on the Super Round Up ride at the adventure park. Colors blurred. Concerned voices merged until they were an indiscriminant noise.

Wh-what is happening? He blinked and focused in the direction of his assailant. The love of his life, crisp and clear in his view, had the unhappiest and most tempestuous expression distorting her gorgeous face. *How is it everything and everyone but Tresa is indistinct? And why is she clothed like that? She shouldn't be dressed in black, but in the vibrant colors of my estate in the springtime.*

Tresa stepped toward him, the weapon poised to strike in her hands. He reached out, needing to touch her, to confirm she stood before him. *She wasn't dead!* Arm stretched, palm up, he begged in silence for forgiveness. *My beautiful Tresa, my love, why did you attack me? I never meant to hurt you.*

She whacked him across his head with the blunt end of the staff. Stars exploded in his vision and his eyes rolled up. He collapsed to the ground and the hard impact of his head on the earth threw him into unconsciousness.

* * * *

"*Herr* Elman? *Fraulein* Grauenvoll has arrived."

Jurgen Elman glanced up from the papers littering his large desk and wiped the ink on his hands on a handkerchief. His butler stood in the doorway of the high-ceilinged, dark-paneled library. Candles shone from strategic places, their light flickering on the shelves of books lining two walls and bronze statuettes on pedestals near the door. "*Vielen Dank*, Gunter. Please show her in."

Gunter bowed his head and turned.

"Oh, and Gunter?"

The butler faced him again. "Lord?"

"Fix your cravat and wipe your cheek." He motioned to his neck, pretending to smooth down a piece of cloth, then mimed wiping his face.

A pale red blush stole over Gunter's balding head. He tidied his formal uniform and removed a stain of color from his skin with quick motions. "Sorry, Sir. I shall show the *Fraulein* in."

Lord Elman chuckled and walked to the French doors behind his desk. He moved the heavy velvet curtains and tied them into place. Afternoon sunlight streaming over the stone balcony and through the tall glass panes illuminated the dour area.

The fruit trees dotting the back forty of the estate bloomed white and pink. Flowers of all kinds and in every color of the rainbow blossomed in the garden that surrounded the tall, evergreen bush maze near the house. Springtime was in full swing. He did not mind Gunter courting Madeline Schmidt, the head cook, or that one of his stable hands sought the favors of one of his maids, but he would have to talk to his staff about their frolicking behavior while they were on duty.

He rubbed his chin. His home and staff required a woman's touch and in a few weeks time they would receive the care and attention they deserved. He and his staff anticipated his upcoming nuptials to Tresa Grauenvoll with pleasure.

"*Fraulein* Grauenvoll."

Jurgen turned from the doors. Gunter stood rigid and sober next to Tresa. An underlying hint of anxiety seemed to mar the butler's expression.

"Thank you, Gunter. You are very kind." Tresa beamed. A playful glint shimmered in her eyes. She stood on her toes and kissed his cheek. "And *Witwe* Schmidt thinks you are special, too. That was from her." She winked at Jurgen.

Gunter's skin colored to a deep crimson. He nodded to Lord Elman, spun on his heel and hurried away without a word.

"I believe you have embarrassed the poor man. Perhaps you should refrain from antagonizing him with your impish antics." Jurgen walked to the front of his desk and sat on the edge.

"I believe he needs to relax and learn to have fun." Tresa stepped into the room and twirled. The material of her hunter green gown with gold embroidery flared out into a bell shape. The corresponding hair ribbon flapped against her long auburn hair. "Thank you for the dress, my love." She touched the back of her head. "It matches the ribbon you gave me last week perfectly."

"It matches your beautiful eyes as well." He pushed off the desk, went to her side and placed a hand in the small of her back. "Come. It is a beautiful day outside. Let us take a walk. I will show you the sights of your soon to be home."

They strolled together down to the ground floor and out the back of the manor. Hand in hand, he led her through the flower garden, pointing out his favorite plants, then through the maze to the other side where the apple orchard spread out over many acres.

"What is that building over there?"

Jurgen's gaze followed the direction of her arm. A few hundred yards away on the edge of the orchard near the forest lining the property sat a small gray stone building. Ivy climbed up its walls. Moss grew out of the cracks in the foundation. A gold cross glinted in the sunlight at the top of a turret window. "That is the estate's old chapel. Since the new church was built in the center of town we no longer congregate in this location." He changed their direction and headed toward it.

"Oh, that is a shame. It is such a quaint church and must have been a pleasure to worship in."

"From what I have been told, it was a wonderful gathering place. The building is now used as the family vault. Mine and my ancestors' most valuable possessions, including the gold crown and scepter which are the only indicators left to prove my family has royal ties, are hidden beneath the Eucharist alter underground in secure and protected chests."

"How fascinating! You never mentioned you are in line for a throne. Can we go take a look at them?" She clutched his arm and gazed at him, hope and excitement evident in her eyes. Her auburn hair glowed like the flames of a harvest fire by the rays of the sun.

"Our ascendancy is under debate. My family line comes from *The Bavarian.* He was excommunicated, made king in another country, rivaled in this country again, then succeeded by a great nephew. In light of all this, my family's hereditary titles have been ignored. It also does not help that prince electors choose, regardless of inheritance, who ascends to power and who does not. As long as my family still has our treasures, we still have hope. If those pieces of history were to fall into the wrong hands, I could lose my lands and what little title I have."

"Oh. Can we go in anyway and look around? Play with your treasures?"

He kissed the back of her hand. "I am sorry, my dear. I do not mean to disappoint you but—" He stiffened, cocked his head and stared at a point over her shoulder. "You there. *Alte Frau.*" Jurgen stepped around Tresa. "State your business."

The older, hunched-back woman curtsied, gazed up from her bowed head. "My pardons, my Lord. I am a new *Haushälterin* to the estate and learning my way around." She pushed a long silver lock of hair that had fallen out of her cap back behind her ear. Though her face pointed toward him, her lazy eyes seemed to stare at the old chapel.

"Very well." Jurgen relaxed not wanting to alarm the vision-disabled woman by being brusque. "But the other housekeepers should have informed you that your duties require you to stay in the manor."

"*Traurig*, my Lord. I will do my best to remember the rules in the future." The elder housekeeper bent her knees once more, then shuffled off down the path and around the corner of the maze.

"Come, my Love." Jurgen placed Tresa's hand in the crook of his arm. "Let us find a quiet spot and enjoy one another's company for a spell." He kissed the side of her head, breathed in the scent of lavender. A sprig of the present he had brought back from France for her was tucked in her hair near the ribbon.

"How lovely, but what of the staff? What if someone comes upon us?"

He directed her toward the woods. "Not to worry. I have a secret spot I go to along the brook. No one will disturb us there."

Minutes later a small clearing appeared framed by tall pine trees and oaks. A slender brook ran along it. Tresa hurried to the creek, removed her soft leather booties, hiked up the hem of her gown and stepped into the water. She danced and splashed, threw her head back in joy. Her laughter tinkled in the air like many tiny bells. Jurgen leaned against a tree, enjoying the sight of his love so carefree and happy. He wanted to see her thusly for the rest of his life, wanted to always bring her pleasure.

"So, my love, do you like my secret spot?"

"It is divine." A smile brightened her face, reached her forest green eyes. Her gaze shone with enthusiasm and wonder. She walked up next to him. "The grass is so soft and cool. The air is fresh. The water is crisp and clear. It is serene here. I see why you chose it and continue to return." She wrapped her arms around him, laid her head upon his shoulder.

Cool air, bringing the heady fragrance of the forest and flowers of the estate's garden, swirled around them. The lavender in her hair teased his senses, brought her to the forefront of his mind. The warmth and gentleness of her embrace sent ripples of desire through his core.

Tresa shifted and gazed up at him. A mischievous grin curled the corners of her mouth. She glanced at his lips then back at his eyes. Her love and zest for life caught him in a firm addiction. He craved her, wanted her in his arms, in his life, in his heart forever. He was never going to let her go.

Jurgen kissed her, gentle and sweet, lips brushing against lips. She molded against him, her curves fitting with precision into his, and hummed in pleasure. His passion mounted. He sought and cupped her breasts, his thumbs brushed over the areas of her nipples, bringing them to hard peaks. She trailed her hand down the front of his trousers, the wool taut against his bulging cock. She pressed her hand to the area and he pulsated against her palm. He wound his hands to her back and held firm to her shoulders, not allowing her any kind of escape while his mouth covered hers with a savage intensity.

Another wave of hungry desire spiraled through him. He groped her ass, his tongue met hers, thrust for thrust. He could not get enough of her.

He ended the kiss, let her continue massaging his cock and rested his forehead against hers while he caught his breath. Tired of her teasing, he stepped away, took her hand and led her to a shaded area under the high boughs of a pine tree.

They sat holding each other. He pressed himself up against her and took her lips in silent, demanding need. Impatience exploded forth and, with hurried movements, he undressed her and himself, then laid her on a bed of pine needles. He spread out on top of her, his massive, solid body generating a substantial amount of heat. Her skin warmed beneath him. He took her mouth with his again. She pulled him close, her fingers splaying across his shoulders and trailing a path down to the sides of his buttocks.

He forced her mouth open with his tongue, pulled hers into his mouth and sucked on it. Her breasts fit perfect in his hands and he caressed them, working her nipples. The more he tantalized them, the deeper she kissed him. A sensuous moan passed from his mouth into hers when she rubbed his taut butt cheeks, then the cleft and the tight opening of his ass. He flipped her over, had her sit on top of him.

She straddled him, positioned her hands on his shoulders, slid them down, engraving all the contours and nuances of his upper torso. Her fingers brushed over his nipples and she flicked the tips. He sucked in his breath. She continued to smooth a path down to his abdomen, where his muscles betrayed him by tensing, shuddering and releasing. At the boundary of his crotch, she stopped, gazed into his eyes, gave him a sly smile and bent forward.

Her hair tickled him. Graceful breezes tantalized his heated skin, stroked his sensitive areas in erotic delight. He breathed deep the scents of the air, the apples, the forest and flowers, her hair, committing them to memory for all time. She suckled, stroked and massaged him with her lips and tongue.

"Halt, *meine Liebe*. I want to be fair to you."

Tresa gazed up at him, licked her lips and maneuvered her crotch over his penis. In one quick stroke, she sheathed him.

He sat up, held her hips and traced the outline of her areola with his lips, flicked the hard nub in the middle with his tongue. While his cock probed the moist junction between her thighs, he switched to the other breast.

Her hands grasped his head. Fingers threaded through his hair. Her canal clenched around his shaft. She increased her pace.

"Oh, Jurgen, I love you so!" Tresa kissed the top of his head.

The muscles encasing his penis clutched him in blissful tightness, milked him, vibrated with her throes of ecstasy. He kissed her, rode the wave of his own sexual rapture and released his seed into her body.

After a few peaceful moments, he removed her from him, assisted her to the ground. His breath caught in his throat when she looked at him. No woman had ever gazed at him with such fiery intensity, such love. He parted her thighs with his knee and lay between her legs, the tip of his penis poised and ready at her opening. She gave a slight nod and that was all the encouragement he needed. He thrust in.

He held her close as he drove himself in and out of her. Several minutes later, he gasped as his whole body seized. Once all his muscles returned to normal, he relaxed and looked down upon her. A contented smile adorned her face. She snuggled up close and sighed.

They woke from a pleasant nap a couple hours later. The sun hung low in the sky.

"Tresa, the hour grows late and I have some business to attend to. Will you be all right on your own until supper?" He donned his clothes and assisted her with her gown.

"Yes. I shall be fine. I wish to roam the garden and maze some more, if that is all right with you."

He kissed her on her forehead. "Anything you wish, my love. My single desire is to make you happy."

Chapter Four

*T*he paramedics arrived and Tresa resumed her position near the tree. Ned's friends bustled around him. They questioned the authorities—was he alive, would he be all right? The emergency medical technicians stated he was alive, his vitals strong but as for a prognosis they couldn't say. That information wouldn't be learned until he went to the hospital and was examined. A policeman asked the group what had occurred. No one could explain Ned's sudden change in health, what made him collapse and fall into unconsciousness.

She wondered for a moment why Artim didn't *see* her as well, then figured it was because she didn't know him, wasn't connected to him. She listened to the people's conversation with half an ear. Jurgen's reaction to her presence and attack may have spooked his friends but not her. What startled her were his memories. Still tapped into his mind, she remembered that special day along with him, the deep blue of the sky, the aroma of the apples and brewing cider, his touch. *His love.*

He had awakened in her arms, attended to her with tenderness. After he went back to the house to take care of some business, she had strolled through the property, content in her love for him and with her life.

What a fool I was.

* * * *

Tresa made another pass through Jurgen's orchard, deciding to gather some apples. If Madeline let her, she would bake her love a pie. Succulent red apples secure in a makeshift pocket of her dress, she wound through the fruit trees, heading toward the house and listening to a rider approach. At the edge of the orchard, the tromping of horse hooves grew louder. She spied the rider and clutched her bounty against her. *Lord Waldgrave.* Her gaze glanced to and fro for a gardener, a foreman, anyone to come and remove the man and his horse from the property. Jurgen would not like his rival invading his land.

The tall, husky man dismounted and strolled up to her. His carrot colored hair and freckled pale skin washed out his features, making him appear insubstantial, wraith-like. Tiny food particles clung to his greasy beard. Dirt and clumps of mud from his travels across the countryside stained his clothing. He was a wealthy, well-dressed pig. "My lovely, Tresa," he crooned. "What an interesting sight you and Lord Elman made."

The apples dropped from her dress and rolled away in the dirt. She slapped a hand over her heart. "You were watching us?" Heat spread up her neck into her cheeks and scalp. She fought the urge to squirm under his scrutiny.

"Ah, yes." His gaze landed and lingered on her chest. He licked his lips. "When I came upon you in the woods and noticed the object of my desire in such an interesting arrangement, mounted and riding on a man, her breasts exposed to the world, I could not help but observe. Lovemaking is a beautiful act. One I hope to perform with you some day." He brushed the backs of his fingertips down her cheek. "*Schone, Fraulein* Tresa Grauenvoll. Horrible surname for my pretty lady."

She grabbed his hand and dug her fingernails into his flesh. "My surname is fine thank you regardless that it means grim and appalling. And, as for your obsession with me, hear me now and hear me well. I am not yours in any capacity, nor will I ever be. My heart belongs to Jurgen and always will." She flung his arm from her in disgust, scrunched her nose. Revulsion churned her stomach. She spit in front of his feet.

He seized the back of her neck and yanked her to him. "Mark *my* words *Fraulein*, you will be mine. I am far more rich and powerful than Lord Elman, and I always acquire what I fancy."

Lord Waldgrave planted his wet lips on hers, forced her mouth open with his tongue. There was nothing graceful about his advance. He licked her teeth, her chin, sucked on her lips. The horrifying oaf stuck his tongue into her mouth as far as he could, gagged her with what he apparently thought was passion.

She inserted her hands between their bodies and, gathering all her might, pushed him away. The foul taste of rotten meat and stale beer lingered on her assaulted tongue, her sore lips. She spat and wiped her mouth with the back of her hand, glaring at him.

"So sweet." He moved to touch her cheek again but she stepped away.

"*Fraulein* Grauenvoll?"

Tresa spun at the sound of her name. Icy anxiety raced through her system when she thought about Lord Waldgrave's attempt to force her into a compromising position. The old housekeeper stood several feet away, her lazy eyes seeming to stare with longing at the revolting man. Tresa raised an eyebrow. *If I did not know better, I would believe she is in love with the man.*

"Lord Elman is requesting your presence in the house. He sent me here to fetch you."

She cleared her mind of the absurd thought about the maid. "*Danke.* I will be along shortly." The maid turned and retraced her steps on the path. Tresa sent one last scathing look to Lord Waldgrave and followed.

* * * *

Tresa walked along the riverbank and, like she had done countless times throughout her long, lonesome existence, examined the events leading up to her execution. She should have tried harder to inform Jurgen of Waldgrave's trespassing, of his assaulting attempts to solicit her affections. But every time she had gathered her nerve and attempted to do so, Gunter had interrupted, that old maid had appeared to clean the room they were in or business had demanded his attention. Being thwarted on a constant basis had been frustrating, then Jurgen had left on a short trip and shortly after he returned she was hanged.

She kicked a rock into the water. She should have clamored more for his attention, just have spit the words out, but no. Starry-eyed and awed by her love's superiority, she had been a dim-witted, mute, subservient fool in his presence. Waldgrave had been persistent. After his third attempt to catch her unaware and compromise her, she never left the manor alone again. Whenever she went anywhere, she always had someone with her. *Except that one instance when Madeline needed a few more apples.* Tresa cursed and whacked a weed with her scythe. The plant's aura split in two, withered into a shriveled black mass, but the spiky green plant, though sickly looking, remained relatively unharmed.

Naive idiot she was, she had offered to run to the orchard and pick some more of the fruit. All the staff members had been occupied so she went alone. Her travels between the manor and the orchard had happened without incident, but for years she believed Waldgrave had been around, had been behind her incrimination. Yet, when she thought about it, deep down she realized he hadn't set her up. He had been too obsessed with her, too filled with lust for her, to put her in such a predicament.

Her mind churned. *Who had hated me so much? Who'd wanted me out of the way?* She had loved Jurgen's staff and believed they felt the same about her. Even after years of analyzing, she still had no idea who stole the crown and scepter. She had no more guesses as to who framed her, nor why Jurgen shunned her during the trial and opted not to believe in her innocence. His disbelief and failure to support her devastated her beyond measure, shattered her spirit. All that was left of her afterward was an empty shell of a woman ready to die.

Jurgen betrayed me, betrayed our love. He has to pay. But how? The man had become immortal and she was a spirit. Her touch only affected him to a certain degree on the physical level. It didn't kill him, but it did bring him to his knees. She chuckled. If she couldn't kill him, she would have some fun tormenting the man, make him wish he hadn't stuck around all these years. And maybe one day when he couldn't take the torture anymore, and she was prepared to listen, he'd tell her why he acted the way he had.

Her late morning stroll led her to a natural made, stone strewn jetty under the highway's bridge. Brown water rushed around the barrier in its quest to make it to the bay miles and miles away. A huge smooth rock caught her attention. She sat on it and laid her scythe on the ground. Her message receiver remained quiet, and she realized it had been silent for hours. She wondered if there was no one dying, or if there was a greater power at work giving her a break from her job. Either way, the lull in duties gave her time to think.

Sticks crunched behind her. She looked over her shoulder. Ned stood several feet away skipping stones along the surface of the water. She rose from her spot, reached out with her mind to his. *Jurgen?*

He turned and caught her gaze. Sunlight illuminated his hair like fine gold coins. The top few buttons of his shirt were unfastened, revealing a patch of hair. *Tresa?* He took a step forward, smoothed a hand over his neck. His gaze appeared to search her. Probably looking for a weapon. *Why did you hurt me yesterday?*

Come here. She waved a hand in the air urging him on. *Come away from the prying eyes above and we'll talk.* She attempted to smile like she used to. The movement strained her jaw muscles.

I don't know. He shook his head. *I'm leery about trusting you.*

Please, Jurgen. Let me apologize to you. She batted her eyelids, acting like a coy maiden while on the inside she wanted to gag. *Come.*

Ned walked toward her, albeit cautious and slow and, when he was safe from public view under the bridge with her, she embraced him.

Can you feel my arms around you? she whispered the words in his mind.

Yes, but not by much. Your embrace resembles a fine spider's web.

Good. She rubbed her cheek against his. *If I said I was sorry for my attack, would you accept my apology?*

I believe so.

Wunderbar, *then I apologize for those actions.* She released him and trailed her hands down his arms. He shivered. *Are you all right?*

Yes. It's just colder in the shade and your touch is a cool breeze. If I had known I'd feel you, I would have worn a jacket.

You won't need a jacket with what I have planned. She reached down to his crotch and grasped the bulge there, concentrating all her energy into the spot. *Do you feel me massaging your cock?*

Mmm, yes.

Are you warming up?

He nodded his head.

She released him, stepped back a few paces and freed her body from her cloak. The black garment floated to the ground, pooled around her feet.

"Are you always naked beneath your cloak?" he stammered, shifting from one foot to the other.

Yes, I am. I have no need for clothes. She tilted her head to the side, ran her hands up her torso and caressed her breasts. *How do I look? I haven't seen myself in ages. I'm curious if I still hold the same allure.*

His Adam's apple bobbed. *You're as beautiful as I remember. You still have milky white skin, wondrous green eyes, rich auburn hair.*

Tresa walked over to him. *And my breasts?* She took his hands and placed them on her mounds.

Still perfect. Just the right amount to fit within my grasp.

She affected the best seductive purr she could while he fondled her. *Kiss me, Jurgen. Touch me. Make me feel what I haven't felt in ages.*

A low moan slipped past his lips, and he centered his hands at her waist, pulled her close to him. He brushed his lips over hers, then captured her mouth in a demanding kiss. His hands roamed up her body, plunged into her hair. His lips wandered over hers, sucking, teasing, licking. A part of her wished she could feel more than his touch. She missed the desire that went along with foreplay.

He pulled back and gazed at her with what appeared to be a desperate longing, with passion. *Did that do anything for you?*

Not really. I no longer experience the feelings that go along with love, but if our being together somehow pleases you then it's all good. At the slight look of dismay in his eyes, she stroked his cheek. *Remove your pants. I want to feel you in my mouth.*

He cocked his head, but then did as she requested, pushing his jeans and underwear down to his ankles. His cock, freed from its confines, bobbed up and down, the size of his shaft the same as she remembered it. She grasped it, bounced the full and heavy length on her palm. He shuddered from her touch, and she looked up at him. His hooded, passion-filled gaze met hers. She grinned and, with her gaze still connected to his, gave the tip of his cock a quick flick of her tongue. He threw his head back, a heated sigh escaped from his lips.

She traced the backs of her fingers along the bottom of his abdomen, trailed them down along his hips and thighs, then smoothed her hands back up his legs and into their juncture to cup his balls and massage them.

He moaned and caressed her shoulder.

Guess I don't have to ask if you feel me playing with you.

No. It feels incredible. I've missed you Tresa, my love.

Love? Truly?

Yes, it's true. I still love you. I never stopped loving you. I never meant to hurt you. You must know that.

❦❦❦❦

Yeah, right you never meant to hurt me, she thought and stroked his shaft from its base to its tip, tightening her grip ever so slight as she neared its end. She leaned forward, placed her mouth around the head of his phallus and rimmed the underside with the tip of her tongue. One hand kneaded his sack. The other hand's thumb and forefinger made an *O* around the base of his dick.

He groaned again. She pulled off and blew featherlike wisps of air up and down the organ, lapped it with her tongue and placed his cock in her mouth. She moaned around it.

Oh, Tresa, yes. You're driving me mad. His hand reached around to the back of her head, fingers threaded into her hair. He pushed her face closer to him.

She moved up and down his length, sucking on the head, stroking the cock with her tongue. Her *O* shaped fingers followed the rhythmic movement. The fingers wrapped tighter in her hair and a low, rolling moan sounded above her. She smiled and kissed her way back up to his cock's moist tip, again letting her fingers capture and glide along his length. Her mouth followed suit of the hand gesture, sucking a good portion of it while also massaging and caressing it with her tongue.

The fingers in her hair untangled themselves, and a hand smoothed down her errant locks. His cock filled her mouth and hit a part of her throat that hadn't been touched in ages. Above her another moan sounded, louder this time, and he took over the rhythm of her fellatio, picking up the cadence of the bobbing movement.

She had him where she wanted him, experiencing the pangs of pleasure. But not for long, she chuckled to herself and, with careful movements, repositioned his cock between her teeth. The shaft pulsated with the beginnings of gratification.

Tresa bit down.

Ned screamed and pushed her away from him. She thudded to the ground on her ass. He snatched his crotch with both hands, fell to the dirt in a fetal position next to her. Tears streamed out of his eyes. "Why'd you bite me?" his voice strained in a pathetic whimper.

She stood, dusted herself, and retrieved her cloak. *Why? Because payback's a bitch and I'm here to collect, you traitorous bastard.* She slipped on her cloak, hiding her naked body from view, and glared at him hoping the scathing look revealed all of her stored rage. She picked up her scythe and poked him with the staff. *You're lucky I don't ram the end of my staff up your ass.*

"Would doing that make you feel better? Would assaulting me with your pole fix what's occurred between us?" He rose and pulled up his underwear and pants, appearing cautious with his genitals.

She rolled her eyes. "No. Nothing can fix us and nothing would make me feel better because I don't feel. I don't experience anything other than anger any longer." Ned opened his mouth. She held up her hand. "Please, spare me. What's done is done." She dematerialized.

Ned searched the area for her, but she remained out of view on the other side of the veil. He appeared absolutely dejected and her heart went out to him.

Her body straightened. Her jaw dropped. *My heart? Since when do I feel compassion?* She tried to examine the emotion, the sympathy that had cropped up toward him, but the feeling had been fleeting, no longer existed. All that remained was a cold emptiness and a distant memory of what the love she once had for him felt like.

Chapter Five

"Where the hell have you been?" Katie seethed the moment Ned entered the hotel room. "I leave to do a couple of errands for Jenna and you disappear?"

"I went for a walk." Ned crossed his arms over his stomach and clenched his jaw. He didn't need another woman criticizing him for his actions.

"A walk. You just got back from the hospital with a mild concussion." She shook her head and held up a hand. "Don't even bother trying to explain. I don't want to hear any of your excuses. I heard enough of your mutterings in the emergency room while you slipped in and out of consciousness."

Cold dread iced his hands and feet. "What was I talking about?" Ned's voice wavered with an edge of fear.

"You kept apologizing to some woman named Tresa. Telling her you loved her. That you didn't mean to hurt her." Katie advanced on him, her gaze narrowed, her nostrils flared. "Who the hell is Tresa?" She shoved his shoulder.

"Someone I used to know. She's been gone from my life for a long time." He slumped into a high-backed chair near the window.

"So why talk about her now?" Her hands gripped her slender hips.

He pictured Tresa, how she looked playing in the brook, remembered her gentle soul and kind heart, then glanced at Katie. *Your jeans and that sweater are too tight. Not appealing at all.* He shook his head. "Katie, she's a part of my past. Just drop it, will you?"

"No, I won't drop it. A part of your past, huh?" She raised a thick, pencil-lined eyebrow. "Not that *far* past you're trying to get me to believe you're from. Is she one of your *spirit* buddies, too?"

Ned rubbed a hand over his face. Fatigue overcame him. His balls and cock ached. He really didn't want to discuss what happened all those centuries ago, nor how he became the judging god. Not while he felt like crap. "I should have never tried to tell you about mine and Artim's immortality."

"Yeah, you're right, because it's all a bunch of bullshit. And I can't believe I'm the one seeing a shrink." She grabbed her purse from the table next to Ned and her leather jacket from a chair. "I have to go out with Jenna, and her cousin Jill, for some last minute wedding items. And Artim's expecting you, too, for whatever it is you guys are planning in the park. I'll see you later." She stepped out of the room and slammed the door behind her.

He rose from the chair like an arthritic old man. His head and cock throbbed in syncopated beats, discomforts due to Tresa. He spied his pain medication on the nightstand and took a dose. Somehow he had to talk to Tresa, convince her he was sorry, without getting injured. Artim would have some good advice, but he didn't want to bother him. The last thing his friend needed during his wedding was to worry about his best man and a Grim Reaper who kept attacking him. Minutes passed as he sat in the chair with his eyes closed. The aches in his body eased and he went to find his friend.

* * * *

Tired, hungry and craving a shower, Ned returned to the hotel room to find it swathed in dim lighting and Katie sprawled on the bed in a provocative pose. Two wine glasses, one full and one half empty, flanked a bottle of wine on the night stand. Rose petals created a path to the bed and the fragrant scent of the plucked flowers hung in the air.

"Katie? What's all this?" He removed his jacket, tossed it onto a chair next to the round table but kept his place near the door. "I thought you were mad at me."

She stood. Her tiny black negligee left nothing for the imagination. "I was. I'm sorry. It's been a little stressful lately." She picked up the less full wine glass and finished the contents. "Plus, I realized I had forgotten to take my meds. So I did. Now all's right with the world." She giggled and twirled the glass in her hand.

"Should you be drinking while you're on medication?" He glanced at the container of pills, at the glass, then her eyes. A small bead of tender concern slipped into his mind.

Katie placed the glass back on the stand and sauntered toward him. "It's all right. The alcohol just intensifies the effects." She trailed a long bright red fingernail down the front of his shirt, lowered a strap of her teddy. "Now about my apology."

Ned gazed down at the petite woman, thought about Tresa and her curvaceous body. Until he'd seen Tresa again, he had forgotten how much he liked women with shape, form and height and wondered how he had been attracted to dainty Katie. Her firecracker personality, he told himself. But that quality had worn thin quick. The woman was high-maintenance in the emotions department. He stayed with her though because she was a friend of Jenna's, he's a friend of Artim's, and together they all had a good time. However, one on one with her had turned out to be a different story.

He missed the old Tresa's good-natured approach to life, the casual way she handled any situation that came to her. Then there was the new Tresa with the dark cloak that hid her creamy white skin and supple breasts. He recalled the caress of her fingers on his skin and his cock hardened, rubbed against the tight fabric of his jeans.

Imagining Katie to be Tresa, he swept her into his arms and passion overrode caution, skewed his reality. He kissed her with all the pent up stress he felt about the return of his lost love and her hostility toward him. Ned trailed his lips and tongue along her jaw, down her neck. He slipped the flimsy piece of lingerie up and over her head, tossed it to the floor and picked her up. Her small breasts rubbed his face. Trailing his tongue along her skin, he searched and found her nipple, then sucked on it. She wrapped her legs around his torso, her arms around his head.

He caressed her back, nipped at her tit, carried her to the bed and laid her down, continuing to stroke her body, continuing to wish she was Tresa. Katie played with his hair as he licked his way down to her crotch and removed her panties. She spread her legs, exposing her pink shaven folds. He darted his tongue between her smooth nether lips, swirled it around, probed her canal. Her hands pulled on his hair, kept his head in place. He inserted a finger to assist his tongue.

"Oh, baby. That's the ticket. Tongue and finger fuck me." She shifted, lifted her pelvis. "Oh, that's it." A passionate moan rumbled through her. Her hips bucked. Her pussy quivered under his mouth.

He kissed her on the inside of each thigh, then placed his chin on her pubic bone.

She propped herself up on her elbows and gazed down at him. "I think it's your turn, mister. Stand up and take those pants off. I want to suck you like there's no tomorrow."

Ned stood and unfastened his fly, wondering for a moment if getting a blow job would be good idea after what happened earlier. On the other hand, he thought, maybe some tender treatment would make his cock feel better. "How can I pass up an offer like that?" Within seconds, he had shucked himself of his clothing and lay naked on the bed beneath Katie.

Her cheek stroked his chest, then she drew lazy circles with the tip of her tongue around his nipples, laved him down to his cock. She kissed its length as if testing its hardness, gave it a small lick, then took it in her mouth. Up and down her head went, his cock experiencing warm moistness one moment, cool air on wet skin the next. She purred and his nerve endings fired in delightful sensation. Fingers teased his balls.

He stroked the top of her ear, remembering Tresa's performance earlier in the day and how she had bitten him. For such an ordeal, he realized he had no more issues. There wasn't any unease in the region, in fact his cock felt great. Katie drew long and hard on his penis. He closed his eyes, tilted his head back, moving his hand to the top of her head, and moaned.

A cool swath of air brushed his side. He opened his eyes. Tresa, nude once again like she was in the woods near the river that afternoon, laid beside him.

Hello, Jurgen. What an interesting sight you two make. She bent over and placed her lips on him, soft and seductive. She moved them apart, urged his mouth open with her tongue, lapped at him a few times, then sat up.

Tresa, what are you doing here? He looked at lips that left him wanting more. His breath hitched as Katie pulled on him deeper and tighter than before.

I came to see the man who claims to love me. Her gaze flicked down to Katie, busy working his shaft, then back to Ned's eyes. She brushed the tips of her fingers over his breast, tweaked the hard nub. *But he seems to be otherwise occupied with another woman.*

It's not what you think. His nipple elongated and stiffened under Tresa's icy touch.

Katie grasped him with a hand, stroking and laving him with skin and mouth. He sucked in a stream of air.

All right, I'll bite. Tresa chuckled and squeezed his pectoral. *So tell me, what* am *I thinking?* She traced his areola.

Ned drew in another sharp breath. *You're thinking that I'm making love to my girlfriend.*

Tresa raised one shoulder, looked away then back. *But that's not it. I'm just getting laid. And I'm pretending she's you.* *Oh that's rich!* Tresa slapped his chest.

He jerked away, scowled at her. *Quit hurting me!*

Katie let his cock slide from her mouth. He and Tresa looked down at her. The spiked-hair woman appeared confused. "Ned, baby. Are you all right?"

"Yeah. Why?"

The woman between his legs wrinkled her brow. "You seem far away, like you're not *here* with me."

"I'm here with you, sweetie." He stroked her cheek with the back of his hand. "You're doing great."

Katie smiled, kissed the mushroom head of his cock, closed her eyes and laved him.

Sweetie? Tresa turned her head, pretended to spit over her shoulder. *Do you love her?*

You know I don't.

Then I should just touch her and get this over with so we can go about our *business. Yes, I think that's what I'll do.* She reached toward Katie. *Just one touch and her life and our problems will all be over.*

Ned snapped to a sitting position. "No!" He slapped her hand away from the head attached to his cock. "Please don't."

Katie stopped her ministrations again. "No? Don't what? Don't touch you here?" She stroked his cock with her hand then her tongue and went back to sucking on him.

Ned sucked in his breath and smiled.

Tresa growled. *If you don't want me to touch her, then tell me that condemning me was a mistake. Tell me that loving you wasn't wrong.*

He moaned and shook his head.

Tresa held a hand above Katie's bobbing head. *Just one little whisper of a touch then.*

"No!"

Katie sat up, trailed her hand along his leg. "What's up, babe? I thought you were in the mood for some fun."

Ned implored Tresa with his gaze, a silent plea for her not to do it. Tresa glared at him. He looked away, focused on Katie and placed a hand on hers locking it into place on his thigh. "I was. I guess I have a lot on my mind right now." He turned back to Tresa, hoping it appeared as if he was just looking away from Katie. "I'm sorry, but I can't give you what you need right now."

Bastard.

"Bastard."

The tandem replies shocked him. He tried to grab a hand of each lady, but Tresa disappeared into thin air while Katie slapped his hand away. She jumped from the bed, gathered her clothes and locked herself in the bathroom.

Ned cupped his forehead with the palms of his hands and hoped Artim and Jenna were having a better pre-wedding festivities night than him.

A couple hours later, he tossed and turned in the bed, looked one more time at Katie who had fallen into the slumber of a drunken stupor next to him, then finally fell into a fitful sleep himself. In the dark dream-void, he called out to his friend, Dion, waited for what seemed like forever and called out again.

The dream-void brightened, filled with fluffy white clouds. Dion manifested with a couple of scantily clothed, buxom women on his arms. Their breasts just about spilled out of the low-cut, thin-stripped tops of their dresses.

He glanced at each dark-haired, olive-skinned beauty then focused on Dion. "Could we speak in private, please?"

Dion gazed with seeming appreciation at the huge breasts of each woman. "Are you sure? We could have a bit of fun first."

"Dion." Ned sighed. "Please."

"Oh, all right. Later, girls!" He clapped and the women disappeared. He snapped his fingers and two chairs emerged. "So what is so important you can't wait until tomorrow?" Dion unbuttoned his suit jacket, sat and smoothed back his black hair.

"Do you remember the night you and I met?" Ned took a seat on the other chair.

"Yes, I do." Dion smiled. "I was in rare form that night." He rubbed manicured nails against the silk of his suit, then held his fingers out for inspection.

"I've found her."

Dion blinked, raised an eyebrow. "Who'd you find?"

"I think you've had a bit too much of your vintages and your mind's fermented." Ned snickered. "I found Tresa."

"What?" Dion bolted from the chair. "How? When?"

"Let me clarify that, she found me, to be exact. It happened yesterday. She attacked me."

Dion's brow furrowed, and he stroked his goatee. "She attacked you? Were there any witnesses?"

"No, not exactly. Dion, she's not in corporeal form. She hasn't reincarnated. She's a Grim Reaper and gathers the souls of the dying."

Dion plopped back onto the chair. "I know what the vassals of death do, but I'm confused. Please explain."

Ned supplied Dion with the details of Tresa's current appearance. "I don't know how it happened or what power interfered to transform her, but she's now a servant of Death. I can't believe she's here. I've searched everywhere and for so long. Once I realized it was Tresa, all that I ever experienced with her came rushing back. She, however, is seeking vengeance against me. She's so angry, filled with such hate. I don't know what to do or how to approach her."

He sat in the chair opposite Dion, his head in his hands. Seeing Tresa again, remembering all that they shared poured into his mind. The ache of her loss was fresh, as if only a day had passed. His mind returned to their life together and with sorrow, he recalled the devastation, the rage, the shock of thinking Tresa had stolen the two items that would have secured his position in the royal court. Ned remembered Tresa's desperate pleadings of innocence when evidence was brought to him indicating her guilt. He refused to listen, couldn't be consoled. Caught in self-righteous rage at the thought of her betrayal, he fell into an all-consuming storm of condemnation and judgment. It was his will that killed Tresa, the love of his life. He had ordered her death by hanging. All they had together was over in one terrible moment.

Dion shook his head. "I'm sorry, my friend. You have my sympathies. If I hadn't entreated my father to help make you immortal in the hopes of finding her again someday, you wouldn't be in this situation now."

"You don't have to apologize." Ned waved a hand at Dion. He understood his companion's motivations. After all, it was in Dion's nature to want to bring an end to the care and worry of another. "I died that day. I watched the love of my life hanged and then her body vanish into thin air. My staff and the villagers had claimed it was the work of the devil, accused me of witchery. I was beside myself with grief when I traveled into the forest. I thought I was dreaming when I saw you and the gathering of nymphs. The wine, the music, the beauty of your clan dancing around the flames was all so surreal. I allowed it to help me forget what had happened for a brief time. But then you whispered in my ear. You asked what I'd do to have Tresa in my arms again. At that moment, I realized I wasn't in a dream. I would have done anything to have her back. I beseeched *you* to help *me*, as I recall." Tension and aggravation cramped Ned's muscles. He stood and paced the dream area in an attempt to relax. With another pang of guilt, he realized he would need to deal with Katie. He may not love her, could never love her the way he did Tresa, but he did owe it to her to be honest. He had to stop their coupling before she experienced any further hurt as a result of his disinterest. "The rest as they say is history. You told me the entity who inhabited the judgment position prior to me had no desire to continue on as the god. Neither you nor your father twisted my arm. It was my choice to take over as Oden."

"Okay, but let me ask you this, do you still love Tresa?"

"Yes, as much as I did while in our former life. That has never changed and seeing her as, as that *creature*..." His heart surged with a new pain. "My beautiful Tresa, who once loved life, now takes it from others with cool detachment."

"You're making my head spin with your pacing. Have a seat while I think for a moment." Dion sat back and crossed his legs. He folded his hands over his stomach and appeared deep in thought. After a few moments of intense concentration, Dion's face lit and a golden glow cast its light on the tanned handsome face of the god. "You know, if Tresa reincarnates then the two of you can be together."

Ned stared at his friend and raised an eyebrow.

"And if you want her to be immortal, too," Dion continued, "I could find a position for her and she can perform the ritual."

"Really? Is that possible?"

Dion shrugged and nodded his head. "Anything's possible."

Relief washed through Ned for the first time in days. "When will Tresa become mortal again?"

"Don't know. But I'll do some digging around, see what I can find out. We'll talk more at the wedding." Dion clapped, the women reappeared and kissed him on his cheeks. "You sure you don't want to have a go?" Dion asked tilting his head to one of the ladies.

"I think I've had my fill of playtime for awhile." Ned replied flatly, thinking about his failed sexual romps in the past twenty-four hours.

"Suit yourself." Dion winked.

Ned woke up to an empty bed.

Chapter Six

*N*ed scanned the assembly of wedding guests and swore in silent agitation. There was no sign of Dion anywhere in the nave. He appreciated the fact it was Samhain Eve and that Dion had his own duties, but the man had promised Artim and Jenna he would be at the wedding. Dion had told him they would talk. Even if Dion hadn't learned anything new, he still wanted to discuss the situation, try to figure out some possible solutions.

He glanced at the bride and groom who were renewing their vows in the church for the benefit of family and friends. They looked happier than they did during their small civil ceremony in Las Vegas. Jenna, resplendent in her white gown, beamed at her husband. Though he couldn't see his friend's face, he was sure Artim returned her smile.

His gaze traveled to Katie. She stood behind Jenna, glowering in his direction. Her hands white-knuckled the autumn harvest bouquet.

A twinge of guilt rolled through him. Katie had every right to be upset with him. He had been busy the past week with best man duties. The location for the ritual had to be secured. Artim and Jenna had required his services for errands and the like.

Then there was Tresa, who had recaptured his mind and heart, stolen more of his attention away.

Katie sneered and snapped her focus to the couple. He sighed. They would need to talk about their relationship, but not until after the ritual on Samhain. His romance woes were not Jenna and Artim's problem. The last thing he wanted was to upset his friends and the spirits who would be in attendance at the rite. Nor would it be all right to disturb Jenna meditation and have his issues weighing on her mind when she had to walk through the ritual fire to become immortal for Artim. They needed their focus on the event coming up, not him. He shifted his feet, ill at ease with the critical state of his affairs.

The ceremony ended and Ned and Katie followed their friends down the aisle to the vestibule. The moment the sanctuary door closed, the photographer whisked the bride and groom away and Katie turned on Ned.

"We are over, Ned," she seethed with restrained anger. "We both know I gave you a lot of slack for your *I'm immortal* stories, but this past week has been too much. You've disappeared for hours on end. You've acted like I don't exist. And don't give me the best man duties excuse. You know it's been more than your obligations to Artim and Jenna taking you away from me. It's been that woman." She paused, her nostrils and gaze flared. "That bitch."

"She is not a bitch," he hissed, impatience edging his voice.

Katie flipped a hand in the air. "Whatever, Ned. You're an ass. I want nothing more to do with you. Our relationship is over." She stormed out of the church into the bright fall day.

* * * *

Ned surveyed the reception room, searched for Katie's signature spiky hair, then looked at his watch. A few hours had passed since he last saw her at the church. They had their photos taken then she had slipped into a friend's vehicle without a word or look in his direction and had left.

Dion still hadn't shown either. Dion's and Katie's absences raised his hackles and tweaked his anger more than he cared to admit. Music blared from the DJ table. His head pounded. *What about the conversation Dion and I were supposed to have? Where the hell is Katie?* He loosened the bowtie of his tuxedo outfit.

He spied Jenna across the room talking to her cousin, Jill, and her cousin's husband and captured her attention.

"Where's Katie?" he mouthed the words. There was no use in straining his voice when she wouldn't hear him.

Jenna shrugged a shoulder. "I don't know," she returned. Artim stood next to her. She tugged on his arm and whispered in his ear. He answered, then she turned and jutted her chin toward the bar area.

Ned dipped his head one time and weaved his way through the guests toward the public area.

Katie sat at the end of the bar between two young men who looked like they stepped out of a sportswear catalogue and belonged at an Ivy League school. Her exaggerated laughter rang over the patrons' voices and sportscasts on the televisions. He strolled up to her, putting a tight rein on his irritation. She leaned too far back on her stool, and it tipped. He caught her before she hit the floor.

"Katie," he said in as a polite tone as he could muster though he wanted to yell at her. "You're soused."

"So?" She stumbled to her feet and pushed him away. "Get your hands off me. I told you we're through."

"Is this guy bothering you?" Ivy Leaguer number one stood and extended a thumb at Ned while his buddy jumped up and hovered at Katie's side.

"No. He's not." A forlorn expression distorted her face. Katie shooed the guys back to their stools, wiped at a dark stain on her maroon-colored strapless bridesmaid dress. "We just broke up today." She sniffed then scowled at Ned.

"Let me take you back to the inn." Bothered by the combined hatred and sadness in her eyes, Ned placed a hand on her shoulder, hoping to impart a measure of comfort.

She flung it off. "You don't have to take me anywhere anymore."

"We could take you back," jock-boy number two offered.

"Your services are not needed." Ned grabbed her arm and dragged her out of the bar.

She trotted next to him, trying to keep up, her high-heeled shoes clicking an energetic staccato on the pavement. The taps echoed into the night. At his car several yards from the bar, Ned stopped short and spun around. "What was all that about?" He swung his arm toward the establishment. "I know you like to party, but you've been smart about it. You've never gotten that out of control."

Katie broke out in a torrent of tears, hid her face in her hands. The blonde tips of her hair glowed from the light of a nearby street lamp.

"Katie, darling, I'm sorry." He put a hand on her shoulder. "I know you don't want anything more to do with me, but I am worried about you."

"Like hell you are," she shouted. Her chest heaved, huge sobs issued forth from her petite frame. She slapped his arm away then shoved his chest. "Why didn't you love me? Why couldn't you love me?"

"I can't say." He hung his head with a slight shake. If he told her the real reason, she'd never believe him. She hadn't accepted his immortal status so how would she understand that he'd been reunited with the love of his life who was now a spirit, more to the point a Grim Reaper? She'd call the white-coat authorities to come take him away in a heartbeat.

"It's that other woman, isn't it?" She wiped her nose with the back of her hand.

"No." He studied her. Black, blue and pink smudged her eyelids and surrounding skin, ran in jagged colored rivers down her cheeks. Clumps of black gunk he assumed was mascara stuck tight to her eyelashes. Her narrowed gaze indicated she thought he was full of crap. "Yes."

"Well, which is it?" She placed her hands on her hips, wobbled, balanced then tapped her foot.

"Yes, there was another woman. I know I told you it was someone I used to know. She's been gone a long time, but I still love her."

"She's dead?

He shrugged.

"So I've been competing with a dead woman. Great. Just great." Katie stomped to the passenger door and yanked it open.

"She's not exactly dead."

Katie stopped in mid-entry, righted herself and looked over the hood of the vehicle. "Excuse me?"

"She's, well, she's a spirit like me and Artim. Well, not like us in so many words but—"

She held up a hand. "Stop. It's been a long day, and I don't want to get into the whole *I'm a spirit* conversation again. You know I had my fill of it when we first started dating. Just take me back to the room." Katie slid into the coupé.

A few minutes later Ned parked the car in front of their room.

"I would rather you not stay with me," Katie stated through a string of hiccups.

"And what would you have me do?" Anger splintered within him. He gripped the steering wheel and gritted his teeth, trying to keep from judging a woman who was inebriated and didn't know any better.

She glanced over her shoulder at the back seat, smirked, then slid out of the automobile and slammed the door.

Ned hurried out of the car after her but was too late. She shut the hotel room door in his face and the lock clicked on the other side. He turned and propped himself against the wall, took several deep breaths to control his ire.

A cool breeze blew over him. He shuddered and folded the lapels of his tuxedo jacket over his chest. *Take a walk.* The unbidden thought stuck in his mind. A walk seemed good. It would help to clear his head. He pushed off the wall and headed for the river.

He followed the path he had strolled down the day before and came upon Tresa sitting on the same rock under the bridge, her back to him.

"Tresa?"

She didn't turn. *Do you still love me?*

Her voice was a sad whisper in his mind.

Surprised, Ned didn't respond at first. *You need to ask?* When she didn't reply, he continued. *Yes, I do.* His shoulders relaxed with the admission. *Do you love me?*

Tresa shook her head and tossed a rock into the dark water. *It's not in my capacity to love. Not anymore. Besides, you sentenced me to a life without love, without feeling.* She sprang from the rock, turned and advanced on him. *How could you do that? Do you have any idea what it was like to be accused of treason by the man who should have been the one to protect me, keep me from harm?* The hood of her cloak fell away. The red in her auburn hair shone like embers of a dying fire in the moonlight. Her gaze flashed with fury and it seemed to bore into him, relentless, accusing. *It was horrific, Jurgen. When you listened to your staff's testimony, the old maid's accusations and didn't believe my story that I was falsely accused, it broke my heart. You were my love. You were supposed to defend me. But no, you pointed your finger and condemned me!* She stepped back, took a deep breath and clutched her cloak over her chest. *You were so stoic. I couldn't believe the unfeeling way you watched the noose circle my neck. You watched the executioner pull the lever and still had no reaction. How can you expect me to love you after that?*

A tear leaked out of the corner of his eye. *I'm so sorry, Tresa.* He wanted to reach out to her, to wrap her in his arms. Her stiff stance though informed him she wouldn't accept his comfort. *I was devastated with my decision, but my people demanded justice. It killed me to observe your sentence, but I couldn't show any weakness. When it was all over, I disappeared into the woods. I prayed for your soul, prayed for a way to be with you again. I became immortal in the hopes of finding you one day so I could apologize.*

She glanced at him. *But why, Jurgen? Why didn't you believe in me, in our love?*

Ned opened his mouth to explain the evidence to her, but a flash of blue light lit the area, drew his attention to Tresa's scythe.

Her gaze fixated on the glowing symbols lining the staff. She picked it up and rotated the rod to continue reading the message. She glanced up at him with a doleful smile. *It doesn't matter. Go back to Katie, Ned.*

In a blink of an eye, she was gone.

* * * *

Tresa stood in a small, beige colored room and stared at a woman passed out on a bed. Her gaze raked in the scene—a pill bottle open and on its side on the nightstand, a half full pack of cigarettes, an empty wine bottle. The room reeked of the woman's body toxins from the booze, smokes and medication. The woman's chest hitched, her breathing grew erratic. She shook her head, marveling over the woman's disregard for her own life.

Ned's not going to like finding his Katie dead. But what can I do?

The staff warmed in her hand. Her job was about to begin. She walked to the side of the bed, waiting for the flames to signify her touch was required to start the dead's journey. She reached out, poising herself to be ready.

The door burst open. She jumped back.

"What the hell are you doing here?" Ned demanded, his form filling the doorway.

She repositioned herself at the bed. *My job!*

The blade erupted in flames. The staff heated her palm. She moved to touch Katie's forehead.

"Don't!" Ned rushed forward and pushed her hand away. He sat on the bed and tried to rouse Katie. There was no response. He turned and picked up the phone on the nightstand, knocking over the pill bottle and cigarettes.

What are you doing, Ned?

Calling for an ambulance. He related the details of his location and what he believed had occurred into the phone.

You can't stop fate, you know. It's her time, Tresa stated when he put the receiver back in the cradle. The blade's flames intensified. She reached out to the woman again.

Ned grabbed her wrist. "Please, Tresa." *Please don't. Katie made a mistake tonight by mixing the drugs and alcohol. A mistake. Let her fight through this and learn her lesson.*

Excuse me? She couldn't believe the gall of his request. *Why should I neglect my duties for a woman you love?*

Because it's a misunderstanding. I don't love her. She and I aren't together anymore. I love you. I've told you that. And I'm sorry for my reaction and accusations all those years ago. I was wrong, so wrong. Can't you ever forgive me?

The flames from the blade danced and leapt, but she ignored them. She yanked her arm from his grip and stepped back. He loved her. He apologized. Was forgiveness possible? His gaze implored her, looked upon her with what appeared to be love. Love for her and not the woman whom she came to assist to the other side of the veil.

She glanced at Katie. Her breathing was ragged, but her spirit fought to stay on the earthly realm. Her focus returned to Ned. He was the man she used to love, the man whose compassion for his fellow man had warmed her heart.

"*Verdammen Sie*, Jurgen," Tresa uttered quiet and sad. She threw her scythe to the ground. The flame winked out, and she dematerialized.

Chapter Seven

Ned stood apart from all of the commotion created by the paramedics and police officers who arrived on the scene. Artim and Jenna had just returned from their reception. They tried to find out what happened, but he was tired of explaining. They tried to comfort him, but he wanted to be alone with his thoughts. He had never wanted to hurt Katie, have their relationship end this way. He had never wanted to hurt Tresa either, but look where that got them.

"My, my, my," Dion's voice rolled deep. "Seems that I missed one hell of a party."

Ned spun toward him. "Where have you been? You were supposed to be at the wedding and the reception. We were supposed to discuss what's been going on."

"So sorry, my good man." Dion patted Ned's shoulder with an impeccable manicured hand. "I told you I would see what I could find and *find* I did. I happened to run into Mors and had a nice visit with him. Of course, I being the great host I am, I conjured a couple of my best cases of wine. Mors, the poor fellow, imbibed beyond his tolerance." Dion chuckled and flashed a smile of straight white teeth. "But his inebriation loosened his tongue, and he told me the most intriguing story." Dion looked up at the sky and then focused on the activities in the parking lot.

Ned crossed his arms over his stomach, tilted his head to the side and raised a brow. "And?"

Dion leaned toward him. "Turns out *Mr. Personification of Death* had been bored with his job of escorting the deceased to the underworld and came to the land of the living for a spell. He'd seen Tresa and developed a crush. His interest in her was so intense that he *walked-in* to Lord Waldgrave. Mors took over the poor slob's mortal form just to be near her. He wasn't very nice to Tresa."

"What?" Ned's voice carried, and an officer looked their way. Ned led him farther from the scene.

Dion nodded. "He'd tried to claim her for his own, but loyal girl she was, she wouldn't give into his charms. Mors said he'd thought his luck had turned when Tresa had been tried for treason and sentenced to be hanged. So, as the breath was leaving her body, he went to her, asked her if she wanted to live. She, thinking he was still Lord Waldgrave, had said yes, if he could save her then do so. *I am innocent after all*, she had said. He'd breathed his spirit into her and whisked her to his home in the underworld. When she woke and had realized where she was and who she was with, she'd grown quite irate." Dion snickered and elbowed Ned. "Always the fiery redhead, wasn't she?"

"Dion…" Ned growled.

"Fine." Dion sighed. "From what he says, even though he'd saved her, she'd insisted she wanted nothing to do with him. He admitted his temper overcame him and in his anger he'd transformed her into one of his workers. It was at that point she had become the grim reaper of this territory far from her home."

"Interesting. That explains how her body vanished from the noose, but still doesn't let me know if she is innocent or not."

Dion grinned again. "That brings me to the next part of my story." He snapped his fingers. A beautiful woman with straight black hair and dark eyes appeared next to him. Her snow white skin contrasted against the black leather collar around her neck and black leather restraints on her ankles and wrists. "Ned meet Aite, my little minx. Aite, Ned." He tapped her under her chin, rattled her chain-linked leash. "Turns out Aite here had a bit of a crush on Lord Waldgrave and popped over to the human realm to have some fun. When she saw Waldgrave was interested in Tresa, her nose got bent out of shape. Didn't it, dear?" He stroked her cheek, and she leaned into his hand. "And, she decided to get rid of Tresa. Show him who you were, Aite."

First, she morphed into the old woman, moments later transformed into a woman resembling Tresa's body stature and coloring, then changed back to herself.

Ned's jaw dropped. He stared at Aite. "Is it true? Tresa was innocent?"

"Yes, it's true," Dion supplied. "Aite framed your beloved. As the old woman, she spied on her, scoped out your property and devised a plan. Disguised as Tresa, she stole the crown and scepter making sure other staff members saw her. Then back in her old housekeeper guise, she brainwashed the staff, made them believe Tresa was evil. They in turn persuaded you, and the rest you know."

"I have to find Tresa." Ned turned. "I have to talk to her."

Dion grabbed his arm and kept him from leaving. "Sorry, pal. I beat you to it. I located her, and she and I had a chat. I told her what I told you. My father happened to come along during the conversation, and after he learned the details, he freed her."

"Freed her?" Cold streams of distress traveled through his body at the thought of losing her again. "What do you mean by that?"

"She's mortal. My father found a despondent human whose soul had withered and was in the process of departing the body. The human, though extremely unhappy, did have a purpose for existing and my father wanted the human's job to continue. He slipped Tresa into the human to replace the dying soul with hers."

"No." Ned shook his head. "She can't be mortal. She can't be gone." He shucked off Dion's hand. He couldn't believe, didn't want to believe, that he had lost her again. "Where is she? Who is she?"

"That I don't know. My father wouldn't say. But he did prompt Tresa to remember you should the two of you ever meet."

Ned sank to the ground, placed his forearms on his bent knees and hid his head. How the hell were they supposed to find each other again?

"Sir?"

He raised his head and through tear filled eyes focused on one of the emergency personnel. A beautiful woman with a square shaped face, strong features, penetrating eyes and dark hair stood before him. A stirring of attraction shuddered in his loins. *But she's so different from my gentle Tresa of old and my current ex-girlfriend Katie.*

"Sir, we're ready to transport. Would you like to ride with us or follow in your own vehicle?"

Dion cocked his head and, keeping hold of the leash, stepped toward the technician. "Do I know you?"

The woman looked Dion up and down with an air of disinterest. "I don't believe so."

"Hmm, that's interesting." He rubbed his chin, his brow creasing, and concentrated on her for a moment. With a smile, he leaned in and at her ear whispered, "Remember."

The woman blinked, shook her head then stared down at herself with a puzzled expression. She patted her body and arms.

"Now do we know each other?"

She looked at Dion, recognition glimmering in her eyes. "*You.* Yes, I know you, and you introduced me to your father." Her voice tinkled in the air like many tiny bells.

"Tresa?" Ned worked his way up to stand on his feet, disconcerted at the turn of events.

Her focus switched from Dion to him. She smiled and her eyes twinkled. "Hello, Jurgen."

He embraced her, trailed his hands over her warm human body. "Oh my God, Tresa, I can't believe it's you."

She hugged him back. "Well, it's me, but not me. Obviously, I'm not who I used to be in appearance, and my name is Zoe now, but my spirit is the same."

"I don't care what body you're in or what your name is." Ned kissed the top of her head, her forehead, her nose then pecked her on the lips. "All I care about is that you're with me finally." Ned released her and kept an arm around her waist. "Thank you, Dion."

"You're welcome, but we still have a slight problem."

"Problem?" Ned and Zoe asked in union.

"Well, Ned *is* immortal and you, Zoe, are *mortal*. Now, you, Zoe, can include yourself in the ritual with Jenna tomorrow night during our Halloween rite and come on over to our side." He looked at Ned. "Or we can release you, and you can be human again."

Zoe gazed up at Ned. "I think I'd like to answer this one."

"Go ahead." Ned smiled.

"I've had enough of being in the spirit world. What I'd like most is to have a home, a family and years of togetherness. If that's all right with you, my love."

"Sounds fabulous to me. Human it is then." Ned nodded at Dion.

Dion grinned. "It's always a pleasure to help out a friend. See you in several decades." With a wink, he changed their fate with a clap of his hands.

Fateful Decision

Chapter One

"*M*y daughter's comments will not get to me," Jill chanted in a strained whisper in the back seat of the speeding taxi.

The car roared around a street corner into an alleyway, throwing her to the left. She slammed her elbow into the broken door handle. A stinging jolt of pain zinged up her arm. She sucked in a quick, thin breath. The assaulting whiff of stale cigarettes and cigars left over from the day when people could smoke in public infiltrated and burned her nose. Coughing and sputtering, she fluttered a hand in front of her face for fresh air.

Little bitch, her mind seethed.

At the end of the narrow street, the driver took another hard turn. She slapped her hand on the vinyl seat for counter balance and encountered a non-descript, sticky substance. Gazing at her hand in disgust, she stuck and un-stuck her fingers together in an attempt to gum up the stuff. The tacky dirt wouldn't budge. She searched her oversized and full black, faux leather purse for a wipe, pulled one out and swiped the gunk from her palm and fingers.

She had told the driver to hurry, but she still wanted to arrive at Ted's office alive. She glared at the back of the bald headed cabbie, then checked the battered, bony protrusion of her arm for any cuts or scrapes, relieved to find none.

Some people! Her thoughts turned back to her family. A fresh infusion of anger fermented her blood. *Her father and I have given her everything, and she tells me she hates me, tells me I'm a frumpy, old, boring woman, in front of her dorm room friends no less. God's sake, I'm only forty-five!*

The car lurched to a stop. A horn blared behind them. The taxi man pushed open a plastic partition that separated driver from fare and was supposed to add a level of security for both.

"We're here, lady." He readjusted a wad of tobacco in his mouth, picked up an old blue and gold coffee can and spat into it. "Fare's fifteen-thirty."

Repulsed by the dark brown flakes and amber saliva stuck to his teeth, she groped for money in her bag, grouped together a ten, a five and a one and held the bills by the edge. "Keep the change," her nauseated voice rushed, hoping the unkempt, vulgar man's stained fingers wouldn't touch her.

She exited the vehicle as fast as her so-called frumpy old body would allow and charged through the expansive gray-slated courtyard to the bank's high-rise. The new modern art sculptures on display melted in a whir of color in her peripheral vision. Any other day she would have stopped to admire the pieces before she went inside. Today she didn't give them a second thought. She had to get to her husband, had to tell him what Elsie had said. Her thick, two inch high heeled shoes clunked on the ten stone stairs leading to the entrance. At the top she paused.

Compose yourself. Ted doesn't like it when you're frazzled.

With a couple of deep breaths, she cultivated her usual calm and happy state, placed a hand on a door handle and caught her image in the tinted window. Strands of her light brown hair, which she had pulled back and wrapped into a bun, had flown loose and tendrils stuck out all over her head. The wrinkled white shirt under her brown wool blazer which she had ironed to perfection a couple of hours ago escaped the blazer's matching skirt.

All right, so I look a bit dowdy and like I stuck my finger in an electrical outlet. She no longer had the body of a twenty-year-old, and even if she did, the grays in her hair would give her age away. She wouldn't win any beauty contests anymore, and she could stand to lose twenty or thirty pounds, but why would her daughter hate her for it?

And what had Elsie meant when she had mumbled dad was better off with the classy one?

She sighed. Her day wasn't turning out anything like her phone line psychic, Tyra, said it would.

With another long drawn out breath, she used the reflection as a mirror. After smoothing and tucking her errant hair strands back into place, she readjusted her clothing.

In spite of everything, she plastered a smile on her face, entered the building and strolled over to the security check-in to the left of the grand foyer. She waited in strained patience for the maintenance man to finish sweeping in front of the desk, and once he moved, she stepped up.

"Good afternoon, Sergeant Russo," she chirped to the bulky, gray-haired man behind the desk. The smile still in place belied her inner turmoil.

"Good afternoon to you, too, Mrs. Burke. I take it you're here to see your husband?"

"Yes, I am. I thought I'd surprise him today and take him out to lunch."

"Sounds like a nice plan." He handed her a clipboard with a sign-in page clipped to it. "Say, you two have an anniversary coming up soon, don't you?"

"In a month." She signed her name and time of entry. "Twenty years. Can you believe it?"

"Nope." He took the clipboard from her and handed her a guest badge. "Seems like only yesterday you were a spry little teen coming in to see your dad, and then Mr. Burke when you were dating. Time sure flies."

"Doesn't it?" She stepped away from the desk and toward the elevator.

"Say hello to him for me. Since it's nearing my feeding time, I might not see you when you come down so I wish you a great day now."

She glanced over her shoulder, her mouth muscles straining under the force of the smile. "You have a nice day, too."

The elevator arrived. Inside the car, she clipped the badge to the lapel of her heavy jacket, pressed the button for her husband's floor and hummed to the *Muzak*. Jill tapped her foot in an impatient beat on the floor, faster than the floor light indicators flashed. With a start, she realized the song she crooned was an old rock tune from her high school days. Jill shook her head in disbelief. Where *had* the time gone?

The doors to the lift swished open. The regular hustle and bustle she expected to encounter was non-existent. The floor's receptionist wasn't at the grand reception desk—the dark overbearing wood structure the staff liked to call the cave. No voices chattered in the forest green painted halls on the left or right. Apprehension gripped her gut.

"Oh no, not now," she moaned. Psychic overtures in general didn't bother her, and she enjoyed Tyra's take on matters, but she immensely disliked her own premonitory vibes. Nothing good ever came from them.

She reached out to the fiddle-leaf fig tree at the corner of the desk and fingered one of the leaves. Rubbing it with her thumb in a rhythmic motion, she hoped to ground herself and dispel her unease.

Her stomach pitched. *Lord, save me if Ted sees me.* He hated the new-age stuff she was into. No matter how many times she tried to explain to him that it helped her connect to her spiritual side, he wouldn't accept her interest.

Jill gazed down at the beautiful leaf she caressed. After the incident in college and her friend introducing her to tarot and psychic cleansings, she had found releasing her worry to plants made her feel closer to the earth, aided her in relaxation. Much to her husband's dismay, she continued her practice by gardening. She had the fullest, prettiest flowers in the neighborhood. She thanked the plant for allowing her to utilize its energy and released the leaf.

Still nervous, she bit her fingernails and surrounding skin and crept down the left hallway and around the corner at the end to the cubicle area of Ted's department. Both departmental front desk secretaries were missing from their seats. No noise came from what the workers called *The Gopher Holes*. She bent her neck and tilted her head to peek into a cubicle. No one. She righted herself. A handwritten sign on the wall grabbed her attention.

The Department of Corporate Investing has gone to Cryin's for a retirement party. A limited staff will return at 3 PM. Should you need service, please leave a message on Brenda's desk or return later today and we will accommodate you then. Thanks!

Wondering why Sergeant Russo hadn't mentioned the party when she'd signed in, she turned to leave but stilled when subdued trills of a saxophone along with the heavy strings of a bass floated to her ears. Jazz music played somewhere on the floor.

Ted loves Jazz.

With hesitation, her senses roused to an extreme state of perception, she skulked along the edge of the room around the perimeter of the cube farm. Her shoes created no sound on the thick-padded silver carpet. She trailed her hand on the available tree leaves of the plants that lined the wall every few feet.

Male and female laughter flowed from the direction of the executives' suites. The man's voice sounded a lot like her husband's.

"Ted?" She cursed, hating how weak and quiet her voice was, barely audible to her own ears.

At the door to her husband's office suite, she turned the handle, mindful to create as little noise as possible. She inched the door open. The music, streaming from his bathroom, stopped.

"Sh. Did you hear that?" A woman's voice echoed from the washroom.

"Hear what?" Ted replied.

To keep from screaming, Jill bit down on the side of the finger she had been picking at with her teeth. The salty tang of blood lined the tip of her tongue. Injured or not, she couldn't release her finger for fear of alerting them to her presence.

"I thought I heard someone call your name."

"Oh, Liz, don't be so paranoid. No one's around. Everyone went to that party, and they think we're at our own meetings elsewhere. Jim's out sick and won't be busting in on us through the other door of this bathroom. There's nothing to worry about, beauty. There's just you, me, and a good hour of uninterrupted us time."

Definitely Ted's voice. Jill recognized the husky, deep roll of his New England roots, and the nickname he used with the woman was one she knew all too well. It had been ages since he had called her *beauty*, an endearment he had used when they had dated and in the beginning years of their marriage. *But he's not calling* me *that now.*

Stifling a sob and the bile rising from her stomach, she took several steps along the wall, finding an access point to listen better. She had to have made a mistake. The man in the washroom with that woman couldn't be her husband.

The bathroom door, ajar a few inches and with a full length mirror on the interior, allowed a glimpse of the couple. She bit her finger harder.

"Are you sure?" With a sexy purr, Liz kicked away the cream colored blouse pooled at her feet. Her navy blue push-up bra contrasted against her pale skin. She dislodged Ted's shirt, pulled it from his pants and unbuttoned it. "We could always go a few blocks over to the hotel. Get a room like we normally do."

"We're fine." He rubbed her breasts through her bra with his thumbs. "Though don't you think being here heightens the experience? Adds to the sense of adventure with the *very off chance* of being caught?"

She shrugged a shoulder.

"I wouldn't worry if I were you. We're alone. We'll be fine in Paris, too, when we get there. No co-workers. No family. Lots of uninterrupted *us* time." He moved his hand to her shoulders and massaged her. "I can't wait to see your beautiful, unflawed skin glowing under the Parisian lights."

A tear trickled from Jill's eye. *Paris was supposed to be* our *trip, my* trip, not hers.

"Hmm, you can't, can you?" Liz fingered the back clasp of her bra. "Will seeing my skin here, under this horrible fluorescent lighting, do for now?"

"I guess so."

She undid her undergarment and pulled it from her arms, letting it dangle in her hand for a moment before she dropped it on her shirt. He grasped and fondled her young, non-sagging breasts with the pert nipples and tiny, cute areolas.

"Oh, beauty," Ted's voice drawled. "You are something special."

Jill's hand had replaced her finger. Pain shot from between her thumb and forefinger where her teeth clamped down. But that bit of discomfort was nothing compared to the knife-like stabbing sensations in her heart and back. Paralyzed to the spot, her mind careened with questions. *What should I do? Confront him here and now? Confront him at home in privacy?* She shut her eyes.

Her father's voice from her childhood echoed in her head admonishing her over talking about private household business to the neighbors. Such conversation isn't proper, he'd said. Outside the home one always has to be the model of decorum and propriety. No one needs to hear about another's dirty laundry.

The warm moisture of tears squeezed through and wet her crow's feet.

"Don't I know it," Liz purred. "You're special to me, too, my big stud."

Jill's eyelids flew open at the woman's seductive voice. Ted's reflection showed him sucking on one of Liz's nipples while fingering the other.

"Mmm, I love when you do that to me. Couldn't we move up the trip? I don't know if I can wait a month to have you all to myself for once. For a whole week no less. It's getting to me having to share you with the missus."

He stood and placed his hands on her hips.

Curiosity caught Jill in a terrible trap. Dumbfounded and mesmerized by the scene as if she watched a bad accident, she knew she should look away, stop gawking, but couldn't.

"I know. But you have to understand. She's the mother of my child. I've known her for a very long time. It's not a circumstance that can be changed overnight. Be patient with me."

"Patient? I think I have been very patient." She pulled off his shirt. "You've gotten three years worth of patience from me."

"Can you give another year's worth? Let Elsie graduate from college before I leave her mother?"

"I guess so." She slid his belt from his pants and undid the button. "So have you told her about the London deal yet and the trip?"

"I told her about the deal. I planned on telling her I had a business trip this evening."

"When was the last time you two made love?" She caressed his chest with her tits.

"Months." He sighed.

"When was the last time she gave you a blow-job?" She unzipped his pants.

"I don't remember." His breath hitched. "It's been quite some time."

"When was the last time I topped you off?" She pulled down his pants and underwear all at once and knelt before him.

"A few days ago?"

"Guess you're due again," her husky voice whispered. She slid her mouth over his cock.

Jill, freed by the shock of the scene in the mirror, contained her scream and fled on silent feet from the room. Her hand was still in her mouth. Her husband's erotic moans of pleasure trailed after her.

Hidden and safe in the elevator, she released the heart-wrenching sobs that had built up during her voyeurism session. With deep, drawn out screams, she beat against the walls of the lift, kicked at the wood panels, and in frantic lunacy, pulled her hair from its confines. Streams of tears poured forth from her eyes, drenching her cheeks.

How could Ted do this? I kept a wonderful home for him, always did what he asked of me, gave him a beautiful daughter. Why! Her soul lamented. Her insides twisted and turned, influenced by remembered images of the woman sucking on her husband's cock.

The bell dinged, signaling her arrival on the ground floor. The moment the doors opened, she bolted through them into a thick crowd that had gathered in the lobby. She pushed toward the exit like a mad woman, her arms swinging and flailing about like she was in a panic to swim to a distant shore. She didn't care what she looked like or who she hurt in her quest to get out of the building. All she wanted was to be as far away from the cheating louse as possible.

Jill yanked off the badge and threw it on the floor before she burst through a doorway and into the glaring daylight.

She raised her arms to her face to shield her eyes from the bright light and stumbled down the steps. At the bottom, she wrapped her arms around her midsection. Through the haze of water-filled eyes, she navigated away from the building, zig zagging across the plaza. Tears from overwhelming despondency continued to stream down her face. In her blurred peripheral vision, she noted how people stopped and stared at her, but she wasn't concerned. Where she went no longer mattered to her as long as it was far from that ass she called a husband.

God, what a fool she had been.

Three years? Three years he and his mistress had performed the horizontal mambo, and she had been clueless. *Fool!*

Her day hadn't turned out anything like her psychic predicted, nor as she planned—a surprise morning visit with her daughter, lunch with her husband, then late afternoon drinks with her cousin, Jenna, and her husband, Artim. She'd give full-of-crap Tyra a piece of her mind the next time she spoke to her.

Superior forces at work…bah!

Abundant love…yeah, right!

Her husband was in his office banging another woman. Her daughter, who she loved more than life itself, hated her. And she was in no mood to hang out with her cousin anymore. She stormed down the sidewalk blinded by tears and fury.

Movement, a trip…sure!

In her search for a pen the night before, the Paris information she had come across in his briefcase wasn't for him and her like she had anticipated, but him and his hussy.

Seemed the only thing Tyra had gotten right was how she'd be surprised today. A torrent of maniacal cackling crested and broke out of her mouth. She was surprised all right.

Kudos to Tyra for nailing that on the head!

If she hadn't decided to drop in on her family in the city, she wouldn't know her husband cheated on her and that she disgusted her daughter.

The classy one. Now she knew whom her daughter meant.

More gales of crazed laughter came from deep within her. Over her laughter, voices shouted. Jill circled in several directions, trying to discern the yelling, and threw off her equilibrium in the process. The bright sun blinded her. The peoples' words jumbled in her mind. By the time she realized they shouted for her to watch out, it was too late. She tripped over a couple of small safety cones, dropped her purse, spun again in an attempt to regain her balance, and fell back first into a gaping hole in the walkway.

Cold, subterranean air rushed up and over her plummeting body. The sunlight compacted into a white disc above her, shrinking in diameter as she descended.

Reminisces of her daughter and husband, and their unkind words and deeds flashed through her mind. Had her life with Ted been that bad? Some horrid nightmare neither he nor she, or even Elsie, could escape? Obviously he thought so if he sought the pleasures of another woman. Evidently her daughter was of the same opinion with the way she had spoken to her and apparently wanted her father with another woman. The thoughts renewed the sharp, stabbing nabs in her chest that she had experienced earlier. The hurt and pain from their betrayals encased and squeezed her heart. Every inch of her body protested the intrusion of the unbearable physical agony and sadness.

Why? Her mind screamed in a gut-racking sob and then surrendered to her body's distress.

The sunlight winked out.

A wave of gratitude washed over her as her world went black.

Chapter Two

*F*irst there was darkness, absolute nothingness, then a black void deep and fathomless, all consuming, cradled her in a cushioning yet firm embrace. Time and place had no meaning, no substance—not to the speck of a creature she had become floating in the *In Between*. She was non-existent but existed, had thoughts but struggled hard to think. Conceptions of warmth, love, peace, of being all knowing, flitted through her consciousness. The impressions faded.

It's begun, a faint but booming voice cried out through the distance of time and space.

A pinpoint of golden light appeared far in the distance.

No, her soul cried. Please, do not send me into the light. Not there. Not yet!

Awareness ebbed and flowed, waxed and waned. Childhood flashed in the skewed state of consciousness. The pretty pink bike with the white wicker basket and shiny silver bell. *Congrats on that A honey.* Adolescence flared next showing the red, two-door compact car with the kick-ass stereo system. *Good job making the honor roll all those semesters and winning all those swim meets.* Young adulthood, college and the apartment followed. Ryan.

Please don't go. Ryan!

A panoramic snapshot lit up. In all directions the scenery expanded, brightened, dominated her. It was her, but not her, sitting in a chair in a wedding gown in front of a mirror. She stared at a gold-handled hairbrush in her hand. The brush was an heirloom from her fiancé's family, given to the bride on her wedding day.

"Jill, honey, it's almost time."

The bride looked from the brush to her mother's reflection in the mirror.

Mom? But she passed away over five years ago.

Gone but not gone, the voice roared.

"Thank you. I think I'm ready." The bride rose, a brilliant smile lighting up her heart shaped face.

Jill remembered all too well that life-changing morning when she was the bride. Desperation, panic, and sadness welled inside her head and soul as she prepared to marry and enter into an uncertain future. One she hadn't planned. Trapped and screaming in her mind and body, it had taken every ounce of her fatherly-instilled decorum to plaster a smile on her face and make sure her voice had just the right crispness of pleasantry to fend off any suspicions. After all *she* had been the one to demand a wedding be scheduled within a week after only two months of dating. To be upset on the big day would have been, well, *not proper.*

But there was no way she could tell her family the truth.

"Ted is a wonderful man." The mother took the bride's arm. "He'll give you and your children the same kind of, if not better, lifestyle your father and I were able to give you."

"I know, Mom." The bride rested a thin hand on her lower abdomen under the hand that held the bouquet of lilies. She followed the older woman out of the dressing room.

In the vestibule outside the doors to the sanctuary, her father took the bride's hand and placed it in the crook of his arm.

"Love you, honey."

"Love you, too, Daddy."

The organ music inside rang with the first chord of the *Wedding March* and ushers on either side opened the two doors. Tiny tears fell from the bride's eyes as her father led her down the isle. Later on people would say it was sweet how she cried tears of joy on her way to meet her love. But tears of joy they weren't. Cornered by a choice that in retrospect was wrong, she now strolled down a path that was not part of her dreams, not in her plans. Ensnared by others' advice and prodding in a time of weakness, she let them decide the best course for her, thus selling her soul in the process.

She had cried for her lost life. She had cried for her questionable future.

She had wondered why fortune had to be so cruel.

The scene winked out, returned her to the darkness, the absolute nothingness. Again the deep black void supported her in its embrace.

Another snapshot, taken in the green hue of a night vision view, replaced the emptiness. The newlyweds of seven months slept peacefully in their bed. The woman shifted. Her breath hitched. Her body twitched. After several moments of restlessness, she calmed only to have it all reoccur again. During the third round, the woman bolted upright in bed, clutching her bulging stomach.

Another memory Jill recalled all too well appeared in her mind. That awful clenching gripped her midsection, the flood of sticky, foul-smelling liquid ran between her legs. The pain, though, was the worst. The stabbing and pounding throbs, as if someone beat her with a sledgehammer, accosted her back like nothing she had ever felt before.

"Ted." The woman shook the man beside her. "Ted, it's time."

"Really?" He sat up rubbing his eyes.

"Yes, really. Now, please help me up and get me to the—" The woman fainted.

Enraptured, Jill watched the event unfold. Her frantic husband attempted to rouse her. He called emergency services. The scene skipped to the couple in the ambulance. The woman was still unconscious. Her husband, a blubbering mess, held her hand and urged her to wake up.

The picture jumped to a hospital operating room. The doctor on-call sliced into the abdomen of the woman whose heart rate and blood pressure dropped with each second that ticked by. Never one to be able to stand blood and gore, Jill turned from the scene. A baby's cry caused her to glance back. The sight warmed her heart. She smiled.

Elsie, my love, my darling baby. So that's what you looked like when you were born.

A nurse hurried the infant from the room. The doctor sutured the woman's gaping wound closed and her vitals returned to normal.

The void faded in and out, flipped to the man and woman, the baby in her arms, sitting in a doctor's office. The dark, imposing furniture and degrees on the wall loomed expansively in Jill's distorted void-vision. She didn't want to hear what the doctor had to say, not again. But whatever force had brought her to this place held her rooted to the spot and kept her ears trained on the conversation that faded in and out of her distressed state of mind.

"...due to the cesarean section...no longer able to have children...possible hysterectomy."

The husband looked at the younger version of her, not with love and shared sorrow over the news, but with loathing.

The glare. *Just another expression from Ted I've become well acquainted with over the years.*

Jill closed her eyes for a moment, trying to shut out the emotional hurt, the pictures the void produced. When she opened them again, the couple sat in a courtroom at the plaintiff's table. Behind them were their parents and toddler. Ted glared at the doctor and the lawyer at the table opposite them. The judge rapped his gavel on the desk.

"In the case of Burke versus Taylor regarding the case of negligent malpractice, I find in favor of the plaintiff. The Burkes will be awarded..."

Standing in the void, Jill threw her hands over her ears. She didn't want to hear any of this either. From her misfortune, her family had become another statistic of sue crazy people in the court system, another kink in the works of malpractice insurance and liability. She and Ted had come away with a hefty amount, which Ted was quick to invest and gain a sizeable return on, using the money for himself, his toys and toward his daughter's education. But to what end? Having more children was no longer a possibility and all the money in the world wouldn't change that.

After the judge stated the verdict, Ted took his daughter in his arms, placed her on his hip and called her *princess* with the same smile he used to look at *her* with. Since that day in the courtroom, all her love and efforts had gone into making her daughter and husband happy over the years. But again, to what end?

Ted and Elsie hated her.

Her soul wailed over her lost dreams. Her soul lamented her bleak future.

The current of whatever controlled her swept her into the black pit of nothingness once more. She demanded to know why fate had to be so cruel.

Time was meaningless in the void. She could have been within the inkiness for hours, or the time elapsed could have been minutes. Either way, she no longer cared.

Jill woke to glaring light permeating her eyelids. She opened her eyes to look out upon the world, putting the edge of her flattened hand to her forehead to help shield her sight from the blinding brilliance. She blinked several times adjusting from the complete darkness she had been in to the new, shockingly white environment. She eased her head to the left then the right, and with extreme care laid both arms down at her sides.

Where am I?

She patted the areas next to her. A cold, smooth surface graced her fingers. Apprehension of what she would find in the new location after her stint in the dark void strummed her nerves. What *had* happened before the sea of black, before clips of her youth had flashed in front of her eyes? She ran a shaky hand through her hair, pulling on a handful. With an anxious chuckle, she figured if she pulled hard enough she could drag the information from her head. But it was of no use. The incident must have been so shocking her mind had decided to block it out.

Once her eyesight had grown accustomed to the surroundings, she sat up and assessed the area. The wall in front of her, the ceiling and the floor beneath her were all comprised of a pristine white marble.

Not too bad, she assured herself, the fear dwindling a little. White meant truth, purity, patience, healing. It was protection from danger. White was *good*, represented Heaven. She heaved a sigh of relief and, moving with care, rotated her body in her sitting position on the floor to see what was behind her.

A deep blue, floor-to-ceiling curtain embroidered with silver stars and the planets in all their chromatic glory hung in thick waves several feet in front of her. The fabric stretched in both directions as far as one could see. She rose, and finding she was steady on her feet, approached the curtain and fingered the velvety folds of the material. The intricate work of the embroidery caught her artistic eye. Tight perfect stitches of shiny colorful threads created the stars of the zodiac, other constellations and the planets. Tracking the pattern of the galaxy with attentive awe, Jill trailed a hand along the drapery as she walked along side it. A sense of calm and peace stole over her.

Taps and whirs from the other side of the curtain, followed by boisterous laughter, sounded over the clicking of her shoes on the marble. She stopped and trained her ears to listen, but was too late. All was quiet. She resumed her walk, glancing to and fro, up and down, hoping to find an opening. Silver and gold rods bent in a slight curve secured the thick blue material to the ceiling.

A circle?

No sooner had Jill asked herself the question, the taps and whirs started again. Upon ending, a spirited chorus of sad, disappointed moans vocalized from the other side. She cocked her head, wondering for a moment at the voices, then continued on, perking her hearing at any little sound. Each noise increased her anxiety. Her breathing sped up. She refocused her attention on the drapery in an attempt to calm down. Though the rich, vibrant colors of the artwork on the curtain astounded her, they couldn't quell her rising fear. Several minutes later, the drapes swished and flung open. She uttered a small, high-pitched scream.

"What do you do here?" a tall, willowy woman with shimmering bronze skin bellowed. She held the curtains to the side by her well-built, outstretched arms.

"I'm...not sure." Jill stepped back, her gaze mesmerized by the beautiful woman whose long, thick black hair was held in place on her head in a gold grape leaf style band. The white, lengthy Greek goddess outfit, cut in a deep V along her chest and open on the sides, accentuated her olive skin tone.

"You enter my domain, and you are not sure what you do here?"

"I was in darkness. I woke up here." She tried to stop the quiver in her voice. "I really have no clue as to the particulars. Do *you* know why I'm here? How I got here? Where is *here* anyway? Is this Heaven? Hell?"

The woman's eyes, the color of the darkest chocolate, appeared to simmer with mysterious thoughts. Her gaze bore into Jill's as she looked down her nose at her. The lady moved her shoulders in a graceful shrug.

Intense moments passed under the woman's silent scrutiny. A new scene lit up on Jill's mind screen. The location was in her husband's office building. A bell dinged. She observed herself bolt from an elevator and gasped over her frightful appearance. Thoughts of despondency and being a fool flitted through Jill's mind.

"That doesn't exactly answer my questions. It only gave me more. Why was I so crazed with sadness? Why do I feel like a fool?"

A disarming wry smile edged the woman's mouth. She waved her hand. Long fingernails flashed with miniature

embedded jewels. "Come. I am Lady Tyche. Come within."
She moved to one side.

Jill proceeded through the opening and followed the
stunning woman into her realm, hoping she'd learn the
answers to her questions.

In the center of the immense area sat a grand wheel,
reminding her of an overgrown merry-go-round from a
children's park. Eight large bars, four thick ones and four thin,
bent up from the platform and met in the middle of the circle.
A short, scrawny blindfolded man dressed in a brown toga
repositioned the wheel so the thicker spokes pointed in the
directions of four light gray statues of various creatures in the
corners of the room. Ghost-like figures with bodies of little
substance perched on the edge of the wheel like thick tendrils
of smoke wafting up from smoldering wood.

The blindfolded man strolled over to Lady Tyche. He
tugged on her dress, and when she leaned toward him, he
whispered in her ear, pointing at one of the hazy figures.
Together the two walked to the enormous contraption. Lady
Tyche took hold of one of the bigger bars and the man one of
the smaller. Three strange words emitted from him. In unison
they pushed.

The *O* shaped eyes and mouths of the ghosts indicated
fervid fear and silent screams as the wheel spun in a dizzying
blur. Round and round it went. The ticks and whirs fast and
furious.

As the merry-go-round slowed, Lady Tyche's assistant
pointed at a figure, and she nodded her head. Apparent relief
flowed over the non-chosen while the one indicated shook his
head several times. The wheel came to an abrupt stop. The
chosen one gripped what he could on the wheel, bucked
forward, and not able to hold his post, fell. Cheers and
laughter rang through the arena, radiated in dense rolling
waves from the large group of assorted mythical creatures and
people standing along the walls.

What in the world did I just witness? A sense of *déjà vu* and keen awareness that the situation around her was odd kept her nerves on a wary edge.

"*Herr* Sehend." Lady Tyche clutched her assistant's shoulder with her graceful hand. "Please reset the wheel."

Uneasy about watching the group's glee over others' misfortunes, even if they happened to be ghosts, Jill turned away. She contemplated the statues set back from the wheel in what she assumed were compass directions.

To what she considered north stood a man with gills that protruded from his neck and back appearing as translucent shiny fairy wings. Next to him sat a wood stand with a bowl of water. On his other side rested a stand with a book.

Opposite him at the south end was a lion, immortalized in a regal pose with a bowl of fire near his feet. A book lay next to the bowl. On the fairy-winged creature's west side perched a bull poised to charge. A beautiful large leafed plant rested next to the animal. The bull's book balanced at the base of the planter.

Then on gill man's right stood a weather vane with an eagle on the top. Shiny neon colored pinwheels on long thin poles stuck in the ground on either side. A book lay on the ground in front of the left pinwheel.

People and creatures she had only seen in mythological illustrations strolled around the wheel. Some paused at the statues and smiled, speaking in hushed tones to them. One or two stroked the all too lifelike marble, creating warm flesh tones which shimmered upon contact, then faded in the wake of their touches.

Jill turned back to the lady and her assistant, who were in deep conversation, their gazes on her. *Herr* Sehend pointed in her direction.

"That is a wonderful idea." Lady Tyche stroked the man's cheek with the backs of her long fingers and nails.

"What idea?" Jill inquired, anxious about the reply. She hoped they wouldn't make her ride the wheel since she was prone to motion sickness.

"I am sending you on a quest. You are to visit the worlds of the four directions and make choices along the way. If the right choice is made you will be given a boon to bring back and show us." The lady stretched and moved her arm in game show style. "If the wrong choice is made, well… Whatever consequences are to be had, you will experience at that time."

"Will participating in this quest allow me to go home? If I agree to do this, will you answer the questions I asked of you before?"

In unison, Lady Tyche and *Herr* Sehend gestured with raises of their shoulders. "Participate and find out," their voices rang in harmony.

Jill let loose a weary breath. If she could remember what happened on her own, then maybe she'd be able to find a way back without their help. Should she take part in their silly game? Whether she remembered or not, did she have a choice? Completing the tasks could prove to be the way home, could answer the questions she had. She had to take the gamble because she sure didn't want to stay in the weird place, wherever and whatever *the place* was. "What do I have to do?"

"Choose one of the statues," the woman swept her other arm out and around. "Go to it and put your hands palms down on the book near the statue. You will learn the rest as you go."

Jill removed her heavy brown blazer and draped it over her arm. Joining the others in their strolls around the room, she appraised each statue then went back to her hosts. "I received a strong impression when I was near the statue of the man, so I believe I'll start the quest with him."

The round of applause from Lady Tyche and the group surprised her. With wide eyes she glanced about.

"Good choice. Now go," Lady Tyche pointed toward the chosen statue. "Have fun and hurry back."

Puzzled over the laughter in the woman's words, Jill frowned at her, then went over to the fairy-winged man statue and looked at the sculpted open book. Strange symbols and words littered the stone pages. *I can't read a damn thing on it.*

Terrified of what was to come, she swallowed hard and placed her hands on the book sculpture. Lady Tyche instructed *Herr* Sehend to spin the wheel. Not caring to see them or the figure before her, she squeezed her eyes shut.

Ticks and whirs resounded behind her. A sensation of being on the wheel racked her body. Round and round she went, faster and faster, her body jostling to and fro until a wave of water knocked the wind out of her and threw her to the ground.

Chapter Three

*J*ill shot up from the depths of the water thrashing her arms, gasping for breath. The instinctual fear of drowning overwhelmed her for a brief moment until she remembered her training. Another wave pummeled her. The force of the breaker dragged her under and swirled her around. She broke free of the currents' clutches and fought the breakers to swim toward the shoreline. With her footing secure on the ocean floor, she sloshed out of the water onto the beach.

Three young women ran toward her. She dropped to her hands and knees in the wet sand, coughing and reclaiming her breath. The edge of the waves nipped and caressed her feet as if trying to grab her and bring her back into the water's embrace.

"Oh my God, Jill. Are you all right?"

She glanced up at a tall, lanky redhead whose long hair was drawn together on each side of her head in thick braids.

"I think so. Give me a minute." Jill sat back on her heels and rubbed the backs of her hands over her face. She slicked her wet hair into place with her fingers, not caring that she filled the strands with sand.

Now where am I? Who's the girl standing in front of me?

Next to the redhead stood another one with the same hairdo, same facial features and body structure.

Twins? Since when do I know twins?

"Like, oh my God, Jill," the carbon copy intoned. "When we saw you get slammed with the first wave and like go under and not come up for awhile then get hit with the next big one… Like we really thought you bit the dust. Dude, you had us worried there."

"Yeah," a brunette chimed in. "Good thing you're a strong swimmer."

"Totally," the twins responded in Valley Girl unison.

Jill lifted her face to the beautiful blue sky. It was a warm sunny day at the shore. Was this a new experience or a situation she had been in before? A strong feeling it was the latter stole over her. She gazed down at her hands resting on her knees. The left one looked different. Jill raised it for closer examination. The scar along her thumb, acquired during a cooking class where she sliced herself instead of an onion, was gone. Her flat midriff was bare. *A bikini?* She skimmed her hands across her abdomen. *I haven't been able to wear a two piece since…* "Wildwood." The word was out of her mouth before she could stop it.

"Yes, Jill, you're in Wildwood," twin number one assured.

"Oh, dear," the brunette uttered. "Do you think she bumped her head?"

"Let me look," the second redhead offered.

"I'm fine. I didn't bump my head." Jill waved the girl's probing hands away. In that instant, she realized who she was with and why she failed to notice the wave coming in. "I just got distracted by those guys playing volleyball over there and got hit by the tide."

"Maybe we should have the lifeguard come over and check you out."

She glanced up to the dark haired girl. An acute longing to see and speak with her old friend, who had married and moved across country a couple years after college, panged her heartstrings.

"Uh, I don't think that's gonna work, Betty," the first twin commented.

"And why's that, Mel?"

"Because Missy was a step ahead of you and went to go get him. Now he seems to be like checking *her* out."

Jill, along with her two friends, turned to look at the six-pack abs, tanned lifeguard who leaned against his wood tower. He flirted with Missy.

A volleyball rolled into the midst of them.

"Hey there," a tall, well-toned young man called out as he jogged up to the group. "We had a couple of people leave the game. You ladies want to join us?"

Melinda picked up the ball and handed it to the man. "Sure. I'm in. How about you?" She turned her back to the man. Making facial gestures, she signaled that all three of them should go.

"I'm in, too. Jill?"

Two pairs of eyes, both with beseeching expressions, gazed down at her.

"You guys go ahead. I'm going to go up to the house to rinse off and rest for a bit."

"You sure you're okay?" Mel asked.

"Yes. I'm fine. I'll be okay," she insisted, waving her hand to shoo them away, wanting to be alone to gather her thoughts.

"I'm Joe. Come on over, and I'll introduce you to the others." He turned and sauntered off.

"Go on." She stood and brushed the sand from her legs. "Have fun."

"Only if you're absolutely sure." Betty placed a hand on her arm.

"Yes. I'm sure." She patted her friend's hand in a motherly fashion.

Betty and Mel glanced at her one more time. The two girls trotted after Joe.

Jill closed her eyes, her older senses raking in the impressions of the happy, carefree time in her young life. Behind her the waves whooshed and scraped along the shoreline. Around her a myriad of joyful voices rang in the air, mixing into a melting pot of euphony. Sunlight warmed her skin. The air carried the aromas of the surf, sand and distant barbecues to her nose. A brief smile touched her lips until she realized what she did. Truly enjoying her surroundings was a task she had stopped partaking in after Ryan. A frown replaced the smile. Tears welled behind her closed eyelids from the melancholy of remembering her lost, blissful youth.

Shaking off the doleful thoughts, she swiped her eyes. She trudged up the slight slope, recognized her yellow beach blanket and fuchsia bag, grabbed them and continued to the rental property two blocks from the beach.

A mothball and slight mold smell accosted her nose when she walked into the four room bungalow. Even though those two odors bothered her as an adult, she missed what they symbolized to her—youth, independence, hopefulness. Eighteen and done with high school, Betty's parents had let them use the small house for a week before their summer jobs started. One last hoorah before real life began, with college, jobs, families of their own.

Jill dropped her stuff next to the couch. She rinsed off in the bathroom. Not bothering to change from her suit and overwhelmed by the memories of her youth, she went back to the living room and collapsed upon the couch. The tears flowed and she fell into a fitful sleep.

"Hello?"

Stirring to the rapping and tapping on metal and the inquiry, she sat up and faced the voice. A young woman stood at the screen door peering into the house.

"Oh, there you are, Jill. May I come in?"

"Sure." She watched the petite, yet buxom blonde dressed in a neon orange bikini and mint green sarong enter and approach her. Jill's memory strained for some idea of who the light haired girl was.

"I ran into your friends. They're going with the guys to the Boardwalk to check out the rides and play some putt-putt. They told me what happened and asked if I could look in on you. You know, make sure you're all right. They said they probably won't be back for a few hours. So, how ya feelin'?"

"I'm okay. You want to sit?" She moved to the end of the small couch. As the girl came around to take a seat, she caught a glimpse of the holly tattoo around her ankle. She remembered Holly was from the rental next door, vacationing in Wildwood with her parents and younger brother. "So why didn't you go with them, Holly?"

"Not my type of scene, bunch of guys strutting around like peacocks while females fawn all over them. I'd rather chill with a good bottle of wine or a pot of coffee and interesting conversation. Got any?"

"Wine, no. Coffee, yes. Conversation, sure."

"Cool. Sit tight. I'll brew us some java and we'll have a girls' night in." Holly patted her leg a couple of times. She bounded off the couch and into the adjoining kitchen. Several minutes later she came back, tray in hand, laden with coffee pot, mugs, creamer and sugar. She set it on the coffee table and poured two cups. "Cream or sugar?"

"Both please." Guilt tugged at the corner of her mind while Holly made the drinks. "You know I should be the one playing hostess. You are the guest in my house, after all."

"Nah, don't worry about it. It's my pleasure."

Holly laid her hand on her leg, stroking her skin a handful of seconds longer than necessary. An uncomfortable warmth spread through Jill.

"Besides," the blond continued, handing her a mug. "You need to rest after getting pummeled in the water like clothes in a washing machine."

"It wasn't *that* bad out there." She took a sip of the coffee. "This is really good."

"Glad you like it." Holly stirred the ingredients in her cup, tapped the spoon on the rim. She set the spoon aside. "So, what are you studying in school?"

"I don't start attending Montclair until the fall, but I plan to major in Fine Arts for Education. You?"

"I finished college this past spring, majored in History." Holly put down her mug and repositioned herself on the couch. "You know, I have to be honest with you. I know I mentioned I wanted conversation, but that wasn't totally true."

"No?" Jill inquired quietly, unease over Holly's behavior heightening. She inched back on the couch toward the armrest to put some distance between them. Allowing her subconscious to open and take an objective look at the situation, the memory of the event dawned in Jill's mind. Holly was the girl she almost had a female sex experience with, but she had chickened out. Not experimenting with Holly was a decision she had looked back on over the years with a bit of regret.

Several snaps clicked nearby. Her heart froze while an image of the spinning wheel revolved in her mind.

"You okay, Jill?"

Jill's focus centered back on the girl. Holly cracked a piece of gum in her mouth.

"Yeah, I'm all right," Jill replied with a slight shake of her head to clear it. "Think I got a bit too much sun today, that's all."

"You poor thing." Holly scooted toward her, reached out and stroked her hair. "I should let you rest, but I can't. Not until I've said what I've come here to say." She cupped Jill's cheek in her palm. "I'm attracted to you. I've gone nuts the past couple of days trying to figure out if I should tell you or not, but I figured it was worth a shot. I know if we were to hook up we'd only have a short time together while we're here on vacation." Holly took her hands in hers. "But that's all right. Some time with you would be better than none at all, right?"

The girl's pleading and hopeful green-eyed gaze pulled at Jill's heartstrings. It was at this point in the exchange that she had turned Holly down in no uncertain terms, informing her that she never had and never would consider sleeping with another woman. She'd been pretty blunt and on the verge of being cruel in her dismissal.

Holly had broken down crying, her body heaving with sobs.

Jill had ordered the distraught woman to leave the house. For years, guilt over the way she had treated Holly followed her. The girl had poured out her heart, and she had stomped on it. She shouldn't have been so mean and unfeeling.

This time though? a voice sounding much like Lady Tyche's inquired in her head.

"Hmm," Jill said out loud. "I must say Holly I'm flattered. But I also have to—"

"You're turning me down, aren't you?"

"Yes."

The girl's lips went tight, created a thin line.

Jill shook her head. "I mean no. Oh geez, I'm botching this. What I mean to say is that I've never been with another female. And you're right. If we did get together, we'd only have a week. I don't want to hurt you, and I don't see why you'd want to be with someone as inexperienced as I am."

"I don't care about experience, and yeah a week isn't much, but it's something. I'd rather have that than nothing."

Jill studied the pretty young woman for a moment, her soft, unwrinkled skin vibrant with youth. The popular adult phrase *if I'd known then what I know now*, repeated in her head, followed by the question, *why not?* She was caught in the past for a reason. Perhaps this was the task she was meant to accomplish. "Well then, I guess I could be your girlfriend for the week."

"Really?" the girl's voice shook, apparently amazed by the answer.

"Really. So now what?"

"Now, we just let nature take its course." Holly moved closer and enclosed her in an embrace.

The girl nuzzled her nose in the crook of her neck, then kissed her way up the side. Holly softly and briefly kissed one cheek of Jill's, then the other. Her lips sought and captured Jill's in a sweet kiss. The blonde's tongue probed into her mouth and gently massaged hers. Jill felt the wonder of the woman in her arms in all her being and returned the girl's embrace. Anticipation of what to come thickened the air in her lungs. The girl's hands caressed her and her mouth kissed her with determination. Hands behind her back sought for, found and undid the tie of her bikini top. The piece of cloth fell between them.

Holly broke off the kiss, sat back and drew a ragged breath, her gaze lingering on Jill's breasts.

"Lovely." Holly removed her own top, brought Jill into her arms again and claimed her mouth once more.

The soft skin of Holly's body rubbed against hers, and her nipples hardened beneath the girl's breasts. A hand clasped her breast and kneaded the mound. Fingers teased the taut nub. The kiss deepened and a primitive urge of heated desire washed through her. Jill clutched the woman's shoulders, bringing her closer in and pinning the hand on her breast between them.

Holly pulled her lips and body away from her, positioned Jill's breast in her hand and took the swollen nipple into her mouth. Jill's hands grasped the suckling woman's head, surprised at the extent of her arousal from being touched by another woman. Her fingers threaded through blonde hair. Jill's hands tensed as Holly's tongue trailed across her chest to her other breast, leaving a cool, sensuous path in its wake. Holly licked the areola, then pressed her down into a horizontal position on the couch. She removed Jill's bikini bottom.

Lips and tongue nibbled and tasted down her abdomen to her thick patch of hair. Hands moved in between her legs, pushed them apart, creating an opening to her crotch. Jill gasped when Holly's lips and tongue took their place on her moist folds, laving the area, flicking and nipping at her clit. A deep moan came from low in her throat, and she continued to grip Holly's hair. Her blood turned to liquid fire. A thick, warm tongue entered her, leisurely moving in and out of her.

Holly's finger entered her. Her tongue lapped and teased her clit. Jill moved her legs a little farther apart to give the young woman better access. The girl's finger and tongue worked her labia and canal, raising her passion. She panted with the throws of passion and new awareness. Jill's hips jerked, and she groaned in mounting pleasure. Small spasms raced through her core as Holly continued to stroke and lave her.

Holly paused, glanced up at her with her big green eyes from her place between her legs. "It's okay, Jill. You can let go. Enjoy the ride." She went back to her task of pleasuring her.

Jill rode Holly's tongue and finger, taking all the girl had to offer and hoping for more. Tremors raced up her torso, pushed her into rapture. She clutched the cushions of the couch, unable to still her moans, while gratifying waves of release shook her to her core.

The girl chuckled, trailed her tongue up her body. Holly kissed her on the chin. "You liked that, didn't you?"

"Yeah, I did. Now it's your turn, right?" Jill inquired, still a bit breathless and excited, looking at Holly's busty chest with its dusty rose peaks.

"Only if you desire."

Jill trailed her fingers along both mounds, the skin silky, and brushed her thumbs over the nipples. She cupped a breast in each hand, bent forward and took one of the rosy tips into her mouth. Another thrill of arousal raced through her as she suckled on the girl's breast. Holly raked her fingers through her hair, held the back of her head. Jill swirled her tongue around the nipple, then moved to the other one and repeated the process. Holly sighed above her.

Jill pulled off and glanced up at her. She trailed kisses down the front of her body, removing the rest of her clothes when she reached her lower waist. Holly sat on the couch and spread her legs. On the floor, Jill knelt between them observing the clean shaven area, the pale pink folds waiting for her touch.

With two fingers, she moved the thick nether lips to the sides and lapped her tongue in the center. "You taste and smell like strawberries," Jill said in amazement, never figuring a cooch would be quite like that.

"Um, well… I kind of prepped myself with some gel before I came over in hopes that the outcome would be positive."

"Ah. Okay." Jill went back to stroking the pussy with her tongue. Repeating what Holly had done to her, she worked the area with her fingers and mouth, licking, stroking, sucking. She caressed Holly's leg with her free hand and occasionally reached up to flick her nipple.

"That's it, Jill. Oh my God, for a beginner you are fucking fabulous."

Holly's hips hitched. Jill pressed in farther. Within moments, Holly cried out. The girl's body tensed, then relaxed into a peaceful sitting position. Jill climbed back up onto the couch, sat next to her and cradled her in her arms.

That was the first of many times together in the new past Jill created for herself. The week passed by quickly. The two of them stole moments together whenever they could, keeping their relationship out of the public eye. The day Holly had to leave was sad for the both of them, but neither cried since they had known their parting would come.

Later that evening, Jill strolled along the beach, happy she had made the decision to participate in such a love affair, open her mind to new experiences. Her shoulders released their tension. No longer would she feel guilt for hurting the girl. Holly was a wonderful woman who would make someone a great partner some day.

The waves rolled, lapped and crested on the sandy shore. She stopped to listen. The crash and scraping of the water soothed her. Turning to resume her walk, she encountered a marble stand with a gold chalice on it.

Take it. It's yours, a mixture of Holly and Lady Tyche's voices whispered in the moonlit night around her. A black velvet bag appeared next to the stand. She removed the chalice from the stand and placed the goblet in the sack. She glanced back at the top of the marble. A painting of Lady Tyche's wheel was on it. She smoothed a hand over the area marveling at the detail of the picture.

Before her eyes, the stand morphed into the statue of the weather vane with the eagle perched on the top. Eyes wide in wonder at the transformation, she touched the new statue to make sure it was real, that her eyes weren't playing tricks on her.

A strong gust of wind came out of nowhere. Sand flew up and whirled around her. She squeezed her eyes closed to protect them from the gritty assault and threw an arm up to cover her face. Another strong gale blasted her from behind and pushed her forward.

Chapter Four

"Wow, that wind is something fierce."

Jill unwrapped her long hair that had encircled her head and neck from the intense wind. Memories of this particular time in her life came right away. "Yeah, welcome to Las Vegas, Betty."

The crush of the crowd pushed her and her best friend into the casino. The mixture of all the flashing lights, whistles and bells from the slot machines rang in her head. Aromas from the nearby restaurants overpowered her. Jill pulled Betty to the side of the grand entrance and out of the throng of tourists so they could get their bearings after their hot, dusty beating outside. She led her over to the galleria bar and ordered them a couple of beers.

"It's so cool that your parents gave you this trip for your twenty-first birthday." Betty took a swig of beer. "Too bad about the storms and wind coming in though."

"Yeah. The wind and all the dust make it kind of hard to sit out at the pool. That's what we get for coming during monsoon season. But a free trip is a free trip." She toasted Betty with her beer. "Let's go see if our favorite machines are available."

Jill spun from the bar and took a step into a brick wall. At least the tall, gorgeous male felt like brick wall. She gazed up into an amazing pair of blue eyes. "I'm so sorry. I didn't mean to run into you like that."

"It's all right. No harm no foul. I'm Deston." He held out one hand and with the other brushed his dark blond hair out of his eyes.

She accepted the handshake. "I'm Jill and that's Betty," she said with a tilt of her head in her friend's direction.

"Hey, Des," a dark haired fellow hollered. The newcomer ran up and slapped a hand on Deston's shoulder. "The table is hot now. You've gotta come back."

"Yeah, in a sec. Ty, this is Jill and Betty."

"Nice to meet you. Come on, Des. The dice won't wait." Ty dashed back to the craps table.

Jill watched Betty's gaze follow Ty. Betty had one of the sappiest smiles she had ever seen on her face.

"Are you ladies busy later?"

"No. We're free," Jill replied since Betty's attention was occupied elsewhere. "What did you have in mind?"

"Dinner, dancing, maybe some gambling. Ty and I can meet you back here," he looked at his watch, "say around seven?"

"Sure. Sounds good."

Des hurried after his friend.

Betty grabbed her arm. "Oh my God, Jill. Did you see that guy? He is absolutely scrumptious."

"They both are, Betts, and we have dates with them tonight."

Betty jumped up and down clapping her hands like a little girl who had just won a prize at a fair.

Later that evening, she and Betty met the men down at the bar and went to dinner at one of the nicer restaurants in the Roman themed casino.

Unfortunately, *older* Jill had trouble remembering the incident with the men and figured she'd have to keep her guard up.

Betty was completely enamored of Ty, an actor from California whose real name was William Tyrell. The two of them had an instant connection and couldn't keep their eyes off each other. Deston on the other hand, though a gentleman, had an air about him Jill couldn't quite put her finger on. He, too, was an actor, in town from Los Angeles for the weekend with his buddies celebrating a commercial spot he had landed. He had made her laugh, was easy to converse with, but seemed too sure of himself which made opening up to him a bit hard. Her older self tagged him as being too self-confident, a bit of a megalomaniac, and very cocky.

"Jill, you wouldn't mind if I stole your friend away for awhile, would you?" Ty inquired once dinner was over.

"No. You two go off and have a good time. I'll catch up with you later, Ty," Deston answered for her.

An alarm shot off in her younger mind warning her that Deston might not be a nice guy after all and her older self agreed. "Um, sure," she replied with a glare at Des. "That is if Betty wants to go." Jill gazed at her friend attempting to communicate that she wanted her to stick around. It was no use. Betty was too wrapped up in her new beau.

With their gazes still locked on each other's, Betty and Ty left the restaurant.

Jill watched her friend leave remembering that Betty was in good hands. She and William had ended up dating long distance while Betty finished college and then married soon after. As for herself, she was in an awkward situation, not being able to remember what happened.

"So how about we go up to my room and have a couple of drinks before we go to the nightclub?"

Knowing she had to see her way through to the end of the event and figure out what Lady Tyche wanted from her on this part of the quest, she answered, "Sure."

Up in the room, Deston fixed a couple of rum and cokes from the mini bar and offered her a seat on the small sofa. He swallowed his drink in one gulp and placed the empty glass on the table next to him. Before she had a chance to take a second sip of her drink, he took the glass from her hands and put it on the table next to his. He kissed her.

His mouth had come in and attached to hers so fast she hadn't had time to blink. Her first instinct was to push him away, but his kiss, persuasive in its insistence, sent her nerves firing off in a fireworks display. She curled her toes in her high heeled shoes and gave into his demands by opening her mouth. His tongue tasted and caressed hers. The lingering sweet traces of the dark rum and soda added to the tongue fest. She sank into his arms.

After several moments, she broke the lip lock and took a deep breath. Dazed, she smiled at him. "Wow. That was something."

"That's not the only thing I'm good at," he said in a deep, heady voice and reclaimed her lips.

Deston's mouth devoured hers in ravishing hunger. One hand reached between them, undid some of the buttons on her blouse and edged inside to stroke the top of her breast. The other hand picked hers up and placed it on the hard bulge in his pants.

She grasped what he offered. "Oh, um, I'm not sure about this, Des." Her tone was playful, flirty. She'd never had a one night stand before, and she was on vacation.

"We don't have to go all the way. Just a little blow job will do me fine. How about it, sweetie?"

"If you're up for a little fun, I'm game." She unzipped him and slipped her fingers into his pants. "Commando, eh?"

Deston sucked in a stream of air and nodded.

Jill sought and found his lips with hers. She forced his mouth open and probed it with her tongue, pressing her body against his and moving him toward the bed. His legs hit the edge and he fell back onto the mattress, his feet still on the floor. She followed him down not breaking the contact of their mouths. With the passion of a young adult, she suckled on his tongue, nipped at his lips.

Jill broke off the kiss and moved down his body, grabbing his pants and pulling them down his taut, toned legs. When his pants and shoes were removed, she tossed them to the side. His erect penis swayed in the air. He moved his hands behind his head to prop it up and smiled at her as she gazed upon his face.

She focused again on his long, thick shaft. Her nerves fluttered with excitement. She bent to his crotch and stopped when the sound of metal clicks ratcheted around her. *The wheel.* Her mind froze and her heart caught in her chest. *Am I ever going to get used to that sound?* She gazed up at the ceiling, caught her breath and calmed her racing pulse. Expecting to see Lady Tyche and her entourage when she glanced about the room, she breathed a sigh of relief when she realized noise came from a cart in the hall that made the atrocious clacking sound.

Oh, if I only knew then, Lady Tyche's voice sighed mockingly in the air around her.

True, Jill agreed. If only I did know in my twenties what I know in my forties.

The memory of the night flared in her mind. She had fellated him, he'd eaten her out and they had a few rounds of sex. He'd mentioned wanting to take her back to LA. She reminded him it was just a fling, no ties. Later they'd gone to the nightclub.

It wasn't until she returned home at the end of the week that she realized he'd given her something more than a fling and memories.

"Baby? Whatcha waiting for?" Des's hooded gaze stared down at her.

"I don't know. I don't think I should." Jill rose and stepped away from the half-naked male.

"What? Why? Are you seeing anyone back in… Where did you say you were from? New Jersey?"

"Actually I am. His name's Steve and we're—"

"You know what? I don't want to hear it." He rose from the bed, hiked up and secured his pants and fixed himself another drink. "Forget about the rest of the date. I just want you to leave."

"Excuse me?" she asked, wondering why he was mad all of the sudden. She buttoned her blouse.

"Leave. Get out of my room. I don't want to scam on another guy's chick." Des fixed another drink and slugged it down.

"But—"

"Just get out." He didn't bother to turn around as she left the room.

Outside in the hall, she leaned against the wall next to his hotel room door and crossed her arms over her stomach. She contemplated telling him he needed to get checked by a doctor, but how would she explain how she knew he was a carrier? Maybe she'd mention something to his friend if their failed tryst came up in conversation. Disappointment waved through her. Cocky as he was, Deston was a hunk, a great kisser and her younger self was still attracted to him. He had filled her with a strange inner excitement that she had wanted to explore more and back then she had.

She pushed off the wall and walked away from the room, bummed her evening had ended so soon, but with the knowledge that it was better to be safe than sorry.

The next morning Betty and Jill waited for Betty's vacation boyfriend outside the buffet area. When Betty saw Ty she jumped into his arms and gave him a huge kiss. Jill tilted her head and furrowed her brow. Des stood nearby and didn't seem too happy.

Confused, she didn't want to say anything or do anything quite yet. This was a whole new situation. Back in the original event, only Ty had come to breakfast and then spent the day with them at the pool. Ty hadn't explained Des's absence and she had never asked about it.

"What's up?" she asked when Des finally walked up next to her, concern hung in her voice over the change in the scenario.

"I got a call and I have to get back to LA as soon as I can. That means I have to miss breakfast." He handed her a large bag from the gift shop. "I wanted to say I'm sorry about being a dick last night. You're a cool chick, and I shouldn't have treated you like I did. Here's a little token marking my apology."

Jill took the bag from him, opened it and peered in. A foot and a half long toy sword sat inside. "Interesting, but cute." She glanced up from the bag. The world around her shimmered, seemed translucent, dreamlike.

"I know. Not exactly a girly thing, but I wanted you to have a reminder to be on the look out for your true knight in shining armor. The soldier who will come along and slay your dragons and steal your heart. You're a great girl and deserve a man who will do that for you."

Stunned, she gazed up at him with wide eyes. *Where's my cocky, self-serving Des from last night?* She reached up with her free hand and stroked his cheek. "That's very sweet of you, Deston. Thank you and thank you for the gift."

He appeared about to say something when the world around her froze. People stopped in mid-stride, mid-sentence, mid-throw of the dice. Her gaze darted around taking in the silent, unmoving world until the marble stand and black bag materialized before her.

The bag the gift was in broke. The sword, having turned into a real blade and grown heavy, fell to the ground. She hefted it from the floor, and in the black bag at the foot of the stand, found a sheath. After sliding the sword into its cover, she placed the item in the velvet sack with the chalice. She put her arm through the drawstring of the bag and fed it up to her shoulder to carry it. Moments later the marble stand morphed into the bull statue. She looked around the casino one last time, said a silent good-bye to Betty, Ty and Des, and put her hands on the stone book.

The people and building faded from view. She emerged into a forest.

A shriek rent the night.

Chapter Five

*J*ill's head shot up, her gaze searching for the cause of the high pitched screech. She jumped backward, landing in a puddle of mud. A large black bird, perched several feet above her on a thick tree limb, squawked. Its black, beady eyes, full of menace, peered down at her. With one flap, its enormous wingspan caught an air current and the bird took flight, weaving through the trees to disappear into the dark forest.

A breeze rustled the leaves above her. Moonlight cast alien, scary shadows within the boughs and onto the ground. More winged creatures took to the air. Ground critters scurried amongst the undergrowth.

A shiver ran through her body. Her gaze darted to and fro. At each flutter of wings and scrape of grass and twig, she twitched and jerked. She spun around, trying to locate the sources of noise and curb her wild imaginings of attacking beasts. Her feet squished in the mud. The wet spongy earth sucked her in, held her tight. She fought free of its grasp and stumbled to the rocky edge of the wide path.

The velvet bag of quest goods slipped from her shoulder. Surprised she still had the bag, Jill righted the strap and tightened the cord making sure it was firm and in place. The brief respite allowed her to gain her bearings. She picked a direction and started walking.

In the open, brighter lit sections of the woods, the path appeared to widen like an actual road with deep ruts the width of a wagon on either side. Occasionally, dollops of horse droppings littered the middle of the road. At least she hoped the large piles of excrement were from a horse and not some alternate realm female-eating beastie.

The new situation perplexed and scared her. Nowhere in her memory did she recall being in a scenario that reminded her of a forest setting in a fairy tale. The story of the boy and girl who encountered a witch flitted through her mind, leaving a frosty path of fear in its wake. Jill wondered what Lady Tyche had in store for her. Her body shook from anxiety. She paused and hugged herself, rubbed her arms for warmth and comfort, then continued on the uncertain journey.

Hours later, with her feet and ankles sore from walking and twisting on the rocks, her throat parched from the lack of anything to drink, she entered a clearing in the woods. A beautiful cottage sat on the other side of the glade.

A fire burned in a pit several feet from the small stone and thatched roof house. The tantalizing aroma of roasting meat wafted to her. She salivated at the thought of food and the moisture teased her dry throat. Exhaustion and her absolute focus on the barbecuing animal slowed down her thought process and her assessment of her new set of circumstances. Only one concept came through her haze. Where there was fire there should be water. Jill clasped her throat in anticipation.

She hastened toward the abode. Her necessity for food and drink vanquished all caution.

Two men in white, monk-looking robes emerged from the house and strolled over to the fire. She came to an abrupt halt halfway across the clearing. Dry grass and tiny twigs crunched beneath her feet. The raven haired heads turned and looked in her direction. Every hormone in her body flared in reaction to the two pairs of dark, sultry looking eyes peering at her. The man on the left flashed a sexy, wicked smile, his white teeth glowing in the moonlight. The man on the right waved her over.

Jill approached the men at the fire, overjoyed at the prospect of eating and drinking. Yet an apprehension settled in her gut. Offering the men a timorous smile, she took a seat on a log across from them. On a spit over the fire hung what appeared to have once been a rabbit. Her mouth watered again.

"Would you care for some wine?" The man on the right stepped around the fire and held out a wooden goblet.

She nodded, afraid to speak through her dry throat, took the wine from him and gulped down the rich, oaky contents. "Thank you," her voice rasped.

"You're welcome," the man who offered her the drink replied, his voice a deep, mesmerizing drawl. "I am Dalvi and my partner's name is Renfi." He strolled back to his companion's side. "You have found your way down Aluca Road to us in Demeter and 'tis good, too. The woods are not safe for one traveling alone."

Dalvi's hooded gaze raked her body in a methodical manner. More icy chills slivered down her limbs from his scrutiny, uneasiness tensed her muscles. *Perhaps, the men aren't as amiable as they first appeared. Perhaps I shouldn't have drunk the wine.* But she was so tired, hungry and thirsty the basic need for survival overcame the logic needed to decide what to do in such a predicament.

Jill glanced over at Renfi who still had a devilish grin plastered on his face. He pulled a long knife from the folds of his robe, studied the glinting metal in the firelight. Renfi hacked a piece of meat off the spit, put it on a wooden plate and handed it to Dalvi.

"Are you hungry, my dear?" Dalvi walked around the fire extending the plate with the juicy piece of cooked flesh toward her.

God, yes, she wanted to shout, but didn't. "Um…," she replied in a timid voice unsure of the men's intent. *What if they drugged the food?*

"We mean you no harm." He picked up the meat and took a bite. He motioned to Renfi to slice off another piece.

The moment Renfi came over with the new plate of food and gave it to her, she wolfed it down not caring about poison or how hot it was until it was too late. Jill fanned the air in front of her open mouth. Dalvi gave her another goblet of wine which she unceremoniously downed to cool her burning mouth. "Thank you. I guess I was hungrier than I thought."

Renfi, who had returned to the fire, came over to her again and slid another piece of meat, larger than the first, off his knife and onto her plate.

"This time I suggest you take smaller bites and let the meat cool before you consume it," Dalvi suggested with a nod and a wink in the direction of her plate.

Famished, the first piece having done nothing to appease the emptiness in her stomach, she stared down at the fire-roasted hunk of animal on the plate. She blew wisps of air over it. Several moments later, feeling that the meat had been sufficiently cooled down, she bit into the succulent flesh. The wild animal, seasoned and cooked to perfection, lacked a gamey taste and melted in her mouth like butter. She took her time eating, savoring every piece, and when finished, placed the plate next to her on the log.

"Thanks again for the food. My compliments to the chef." She nodded at Renfi.

"You are most welcome, Miss…?" Dalvi crossed his arms over his body, slipped his hands into the sleeves of his robe and cocked his head.

"Oh, me and my manners. My name is Jill." She stood and offered her hand. "Jill Burke."

Dalvi glanced at her outstretched hand, but didn't take it. She returned to the log.

"What brings you to these woods? Why are you traveling all alone?"

Dalvi's penetrating gaze and blunt inquiries unnerved her. Slow vibrations of anxiety trembled within her body. She wasn't sure if she should tell the men the truth about the quest or make up a tale that didn't portray her like a fool. Choosing the latter, she replied in a calm, strong voice, belying her fear, "I seemed to have gotten lost. I'm sure the group I'm with will find me quite soon." She broke eye contact with Dalvi and focused on Renfi.

Renfi sat next to the fire quietly talking to himself and tossing brightly colored sticks onto the flames. A flash of green illuminated the surroundings for a few seconds.

"What's he saying?" she asked Dalvi, not taking her eyes off of Renfi and his seeming meditation.

"He is apologizing to the trees for burning them. He is thanking them for the warmth and services they provide us."

"Why are the sticks colored?" Her question came just as Renfi threw a navy colored stick into the fiery pit. The small branch popped and sizzled. A brilliant burst of blue blazed in front of them.

"They are dyed with the juice and skins of special berries for ceremonial purposes."

A heady spicy scent drifted on the smoke.

"Oh. I'm interrupting something, aren't I?" She put her hands on the log wanting to push herself to her feet so she could leave, but yawned instead. A sudden sensation of lightheadedness and euphoric warmth washed through her.

"No. You are not disturbing us." Dalvi stepped closer to the fire, removed his hands from his sleeves, pulled some leaves from his pockets and pitched them onto the fire. Renfi poked at the burning logs with a sharp tipped staff. The smoke thickened, grew more intoxicating.

Renfi rose, strolled over to Dalvi and dropped the charred staff to the ground. The quiet one removed his robe and stood in all his naked glory in front of his companion. Dalvi kissed Renfi's left cheek, his right cheek, shucked his own robe and opened his arms. Renfi stepped into Dalvi's nude embrace, his cock rubbing against the other man's cock. Dalvi's mouth descended upon Renfi's in a deep lustful kiss.

Jill sipped on her wine, trying to pull her gaze away from the kissing men, but was unable to do so. Reasoning that if they had a problem with her observing them in their sex play they'd go inside, she relaxed and watched the two men, intrigued by their intimate embrace, their hard cocks brushing against each other's.

The rustling leaves of the trees, the scratching of the forest's animals and the crackling of the fire grew louder. Shadows and light became stark. The fire's colors grew vivid. She closed her eyes to reorient herself, to become lucid again, but her efforts failed. Groggily, she opened her eyes and focused on the men. Renfi was on his knees, suckling on Dalvi's cock. She stifled an embarrassed giggle.

Renfi's mouth slid off the cock. He looked her way with a bemused smile, his eye teeth long and pointed. He turned back to his companion and bit the inside of his thigh. Dalvi threw back his head. A passionate groan escaped his mouth.

Fangs? She closed her eyes and shook her head to clear it of the vampiric images.

A breeze blew the inebriating smoke toward her. Another wave of pleasant dizziness swept through her. She swayed on the log, her eyelids fluttered. Strong hands gripped her arms. The men lifted her to her feet. Renfi nuzzled his nose in her hair. Dalvi, on her other side, kissed her neck. Trapped in a drug-like daze, she didn't bother to fight off their advances. The men unclothed her, and within moments, cool evening air glided over her bare skin. The men licked and stroked the length of her body. Their moist tongues left chilling paths in the wakes of their touches. Their hands swirled in light graceful motions upon her skin.

She tilted her head back. Her eyes closed. She sighed in bliss, never remembering any of her sexual experiences being so deeply sensual or so erotic. Jill grasped the men's heads, fingers entwined in their hair. Their mouths sought her breasts, each man taking a nipple and drawing the taut bud between his lips. Another moan escaped her as they fondled and suckled on her breasts, and their hands explored her body.

Dalvi dropped to his knees in front of her and slipped a hand between her thighs. A finger edged its way between her folds and stroked her. His breath drifted over her pubes. A second finger slipped into her. His tongue flicked her clit. Mouth and hand brought forth cresting waves of passion within her, flooding the fingered area with moisture. Renfi continued to knead and lave her breasts. Dalvi's tongue replaced his fingers. Thrill after thrill shot through her as they possessed her body in their titillating love play.

The fire crackled and snapped in a patterned clicking noise. The scrape of teeth along the inside of her thigh and on her breast jolted her out of an orgasm and back to the reality of her situation. An image of Renfi's fangs popped into her head. Vampires, her mind cautioned.

A rush of adrenaline fired off the fear of being bitten and startled her out of the smoky drug-induced haze. She dislodged herself from the men, and at their perplexed gazes, offered them what she hoped was a sexy, confident smile. "You know what, fellows?" she asked in a husky whisper. She prayed she sounded flirtatious enough to be believable. "I so enjoyed watching you two kiss and play with each other that I was wondering if you could do it again."

Dalvi and Renfi glanced at each other and in seconds they were in each other's arms. In the midst of a passionate kiss, they dropped and rolled on the ground. Dalvi, the bigger of the two, gained dominance and pinned Renfi beneath him. Fangs protruded from his mouth, and in a flash, sank into Renfi's neck.

With the men engaged in their antics, Jill dressed and removed the sword from the quest bag and its scabbard. The shiny silver weapon, no longer a toy, gleamed in firelight. Testing the weight of it, she swung it in the air a couple of times. She placed both hands on the hilt. With the sword firm in her grasp, she advanced upon the lovers on the ground, raised the weapon above her head, pointed end facing down, and with all her might shoved the forged metal into Dalvi.

The blade pierced his back sliding clear through and into Renfi below him.

In a fit of rage, Dalvi sprung to his feet, swinging his arms, attempting to gain access to the sword sticking out of his back. Stunned, Renfi sat on the ground watching Dalvi jerk and spin around.

Jill quickly moved around the men, grabbed the staff Renfi had dropped. Before Renfi had a chance to fight back, she stabbed him through the heart. Both men thrashed around, their screams penetrating the night. Jill bent over, her hands on her knees, trying to catch her breath and calm her racing heart. She kept a wary eye on Dalvi and Renfi.

Their screams quieted. In unison, they dropped to the ground, and in simultaneous bursts of flame, they spontaneously combusted. Their bodies turned into black husks that fell into two neat piles of ash.

Jill crept toward the dark mounds, snatched the sword from the closer of the two, and keeping the front of her body to the decayed men, backed away to the log. She cleaned off the weapon as best she could on the grass, placed it back in its sheath, then the bag. She hurried from the clearing to the wagon trail.

A few miles later a creek intercepted the trail. She placed a finger in the water, brought it to her nose and sniffed. Not finding a smell, she licked the water off her finger and decided it was all right as a drinking source. She brought out the chalice and used it to gather water to quench her thirst. Satiated, she sat back on the heels of her feet and took a moment to breathe.

Behind her a throat cleared. Jill spun toward the noise. A rich-looking merchant with a purple plume in his felt hat perched on top of a wagon. He gazed down at her. For a moment she wondered how he, his two horses and the cart could have arrived so soundlessly, but was distracted by the burlap sack he held out.

"Here you go, miss." He tossed the bag down to her. It landed on the ground, and the contents tinged. "A bit o' coin for ye as a thank you for ridding me forest of those two devils." He tipped his head in the direction she had come from.

"Not a problem. Glad to help." She shook her head, then mumbled, "Though I don't remember there being any vampires in my life."

The man chuckled and bent over with his forearm across his knee. "But there were plenty. Didn't you have a penchant for those kinds o' characters in the books you've read?" With another laugh he straightened, slapped his horse with the reins and drove off, disappearing into the trees.

Placing the chalice back into the quest bag and adding the bag of coins to her spoils, she thought about what the man had said. She did love reading about vampires and had imagined what it would be like to be undead and immortal. But apparently when given the chance, she realized she'd rather keep her mortality.

She rose from the ground and slung the bag strap over her shoulder. Figuring she needed to find a way around the creek, she turned back to the trail and encountered the marble stand. As she stepped up to it, the stand morphed into the statue of a lion. A tired breath expelled from her. She put her hands on the book and wearily speculated where the quest would take her next.

Chapter Six

*J*ill appeared in the midst of a bustling coffee shop. Patrons milled about, waiting for their orders and for seats to open up. Craving the familiar, comforting scent of roasting Arabica beans to remind her of a joyful time in her youth, she sniffed the air, but encountered no aromatic bouquet. She drew in another long breath through her nose, then furrowed her brow. The lack of smell concerned her.

Perhaps if I got closer to the source, she thought and stepped toward the counter.

A customer, apparently in a hurry, spun from the register with coffee and donut in hand. With no time to react, Jill braced herself for impact expecting a dousing from the woman's drink. The female walked right through her.

Stunned, she turned and gaped at the woman's back. A bell dinged over the door as the frazzled female rushed out, obviously oblivious to what had occurred and almost collided with a man as he strolled in. The sunlit backlighting washed out his features. He advanced farther inside, his tall gorgeous appearance focusing in perfect clarity.

Could it be? Do I dare to hope?

The man stared right at her. Jill blinked in surprise. *Ryan?*

The male with the tan swimmer's physique grinned in her direction. The stunning smile lit up his face.

Ryan! Her heart sang with joy, and she flung herself toward him. "I've missed you so—" Her arms flailed in front of her, slipping straight through him. She collapsed onto the floor.

"Must be the air conditioning," he stated above her.

She glanced up at Ryan, wondered what had prevented her from hugging him, and then studied her hands. The fleshy pink of her skin had turned semitransparent allowing the pattern on the tile floor to show through. Her gaze raked up her arm, then down to her torso. Her whole body appeared ghost-like.

I'm a ghost? A cold knot formed in her stomach.

"Hello, beautiful," Ryan's warm and lush voice crooned.

"Hello, handsome," a young, playful voice responded.

Jill jumped to her feet shocked to hear her own voice coming from a different place. Her younger self wrapped her arms around Ryan. Sucking in a shaky breath, she jerked her gaze away, a dry sob burning her throat.

Betty walked into the store, took one look at the couple, smiled and sat at a table.

Jill's gaze darted around the area. Ryan and her younger self spoke quietly near the counter. Betty looked like a kid at Christmas, all excited about something. A loud crash from the back brought all the hustle in the front to a temporary standstill. Frozen in a dazed tableau, the enormity of the situation struck Jill full force. After a few months of being friends and seeing each other in group social situations, this was the day Ryan had finally asked her out on a real date.

She turned back to the couple. Ryan brushed a lock of hair from her younger self's face and tucked it behind her ear. Jill remembered the moment as if it had happened yesterday. The intensity of his gaze when he had told her how much she meant to him and how he wanted to have something more with her had seemed to suck the air out of her lungs, heated her blood. The gentleness of his touch after he had tucked the strands back in place and trailed his fingers along her chin had awakened her love, sent her spirit soaring.

People had been right. When you met the one you were to be with forever, you just knew. That day in the coffee shop she'd realized she'd met the love of her life.

Recalling how she had longed to have the sweet moment last eternally, to float endlessly on the giddy cloud of sensation, Jill closed her eyes, wanting to cry, but no tears would come. She threw her head back, glared at the ceiling and released a sorrowful groan from deep within her.

Lady Tyche! What fresh hell is this? Why out of all the situations in my life do I have to be a ghost in this one? Out of all of them, the incident with Ryan is the one I needed to be in control of most! Lady Tyche!

Deafening clicking snapped in her head. She fell to her knees. Pain shot up her legs from the impact on the hard floor. Jill clamped her hands over her ears. The sound continued to crescendo in her mind. She squeezed her eyes shut, clasped her head tighter, willing the noise to cease.

I'm sorry!

Suddenly the racket ended. Tremendous silence consumed her. Slowly, she opened her eyes and released her grip on her head. The blackness of the void greeted her. A flash of bright white light winked.

In an instant she manifested in a seat in an empty theater. Troubled over what was to come, gooseflesh rippled up her back, down her arms. Her heart pounded. A large screen loomed in front of her. Behind her whirred an old movie projector. Blurred images sprang up on the screen. The action on the panel paused, distorted, faded. Soon the scene she had just witnessed focused clearly on the screen.

She clenched her teeth against the wave of bitterness that threatened to surge through her.

In the picture playing on the display, she and Ryan stood before each other gazing into each other's eyes. Their looks, containing so much love, held promise for the future. A pretty blush stole over her cheeks.

Betty dashed over to them, appearing like she was about to burst at the seams. "So? Did you do it?" She grabbed onto Ryan's arm and beamed at Jill. "Did you finally ask her out?"

"Yes," Ryan replied, his gaze never leaving Jill's.

"And?" Betty directed to Jill.

"And, of course, I said yes." Jill's blush intensified.

"Oh, this is so wonderful!" Betty released Ryan and hugged her friend. "Bobby mentioned you planned to do it, and I've been biting my tongue trying to keep it a secret. Now when Ty comes to town we can double date."

"How about you let us go on a solo date first?" Ryan chuckled.

"Oh, sure, of course," Betty stammered. "You have a couple of weeks before Ty arrives for a visit. This is so great! I have to go tell Mel." She rushed off.

On screen Jill gazed and smiled at on screen Ryan, and they shared their first kiss.

Stuck in the theater seat, older Jill sighed in remembrance. That kiss, though brief and light, had been glorious. He had brushed his sexy lips over hers with a modicum of pressure, lingered for only a few seconds. But there had been a wealth of feeling in that tiny kiss. The world around her had disappeared, and at that time, all she had been aware of was him. Her thought that day and in the coming months had been that there would be no other man in her heart.

The images sped up. Numerous dates and phone calls, flowers, movies, dinners, kisses flipped on the screen reminding her of the incredible times they had shared. Older Jill squelched the rising wail in her throat, fought back the tears welling in her eyes. Handsome Ryan with his golden locks and stunning blue eyes, the perfect gentleman, the bighearted charmer, had been her true love. It hadn't mattered that he was five years older. It hadn't mattered that they didn't make love until the night he had proposed and she had accepted. She'd loved him then, loved him still. Her family and friends had loved him. They had been an ideal couple, had treated each other like royalty in the two years of bliss they'd had together.

A still frame of Ryan popping the question flared onto the screen. Galled that she had to sit and observe another event between her and the man she had loved like no other man, she narrowed her eyes at the picture.

They'd gone to the state park in the late afternoon for a picnic and to listen to the jazz concert that evening. As the hot August sun set over the park's lake, he went down on one knee and held a black box in his hand. The golden sunlight shimmered on the water and cast a romantic hue on them. The white gold band with the princess cut diamond sparkled in the gloaming. Tears glistened in her younger self's eyes.

The picture before her flickered and resumed playing. She sank in her seat and crossed her arms over her midsection like a petulant child.

"Jillian Elizabeth Norris, I love you. I've loved you since the moment I met you and will till the day I die. I can't imagine my life without you in it. I want you by my side always. I want you to be my partner, my best friend, my lover now and forever. Will you do me the pleasure of becoming my wife?" Ryan smiled and gazed at her with an apparent combination of anticipation and nervousness.

"Oh, my God. Oh, my God," she shrieked, fidgeting in place and flapping her hands in the air near her face. She bounced on the balls of her feet. With shaky fingers, she snatched the box from his hands and placed the ring on the appropriate finger of her left hand. Young Jill admired the piece of jewelry for a moment, then threw her arms around him. "Of course I will! I love you, too, Ryan. It would be an honor for me to be your wife." She showered his forehead and the sides of his face with kisses.

All through the concert that evening she marveled at the ring on her finger. The man who made her heart beat fast, who she wanted to have children with, the man of her dreams had proposed. He would be hers forever.

Older Jill tore her gaze from the screen. Memories of her feelings washed through her. Old pain danced within her, blending with the fury of the injustice that was to come. She had been so happy in their time together. When he had asked her to marry him, she had thought she had died and gone to heaven. She considered herself the luckiest girl in the world. Then toward the end of the concert when he had brushed his nose against her ear and whispered that he wanted to take her back to his place, flaming hot desire for her man had raged within her.

The movie cut to Ryan's apartment bedroom. The two of them were a naked tangle of legs and arms as they kissed and pawed at each other on the mattress. Discarded clothes lay at the foot of the bed.

Jill shifted in the theater seat, uncomfortable being a voyeur, but strangely titillated at the same time. Recollections of their first time making love added to the flavor of the movie.

My soul had warmed in joy as I lay in his embrace. His spirit had seemed to join with my own, become a part of me.

Ryan lowered his head and touched his lips to hers. A tremor rippled through the young woman on the screen. His kiss became more persuasive, and she didn't draw away. She met his command and parted her mouth. Ryan nicked her lips with his teeth, caressed her tongue with his. He cupped her chin with one hand and wrapped the other around her breast.

I had felt like free flowing liquid as he brought my desires and passion out with his touch.

Younger Jill placed her hands on his shoulders. She slid her hands down his body, feeling all the contours and nuances of his upper torso. He sucked in his breath when her fingers brushed over his nipples.

God, his body had been a wonder to behold, so toned and in shape from his time in the pool and in the gym. The skin of his chest beneath my fingers was so soft and so hot. His muscles hard and defined.

He was so sturdy and warm. The subtle scent of his manly musk had intoxicated my senses. I had been consumed with lust for him.

Moisture had flooded between my legs as I pleasured the man I loved, and at that point, I realized I wanted him inside me, touching my soul.

After many minutes of foreplay, he slowly climbed up, positioned himself and entered her. He latched on to her right nipple with his mouth. He teased the peak with his tongue.

Tingles of pleasure had trickled up and down my body. There was no pain as I had thought there would be. I had gathered my days in gymnastics as a child had paid off. I had shifted to give him more access to my breast and a delightful sensation had stirred in my muscles around his cock. That's when I had circled my hips slightly and had begun to lose all control.

He continued to suckle on one breast and caress the other. She slowly undulated her hips, letting his thick shaft slide in and out of her canal. Her hips rose to meet him. He delved in deeper.

In our union, I believed he had hit my center, my soul. The love I felt for him at that moment had engulfed my whole being. Each movement, each gentle stroke of his penis within me had increased the fire burning within until I allowed the orgasm to take over.

Joining and separating in a heated frenzy, they made love. Sweat slicked back their hair, glistened on their bodies. They panted and gasped, exclaiming almost in unison when their closely timed orgasms racked their bodies. Satiated, they rested in peaceful bliss in each other's arms.

"Beautiful. Absolutely beautiful," Ryan crooned, stroking the hair of her head.

Older Jill covered her face with her hands and wept.

Minutes later she composed herself, wiped the wet from her face and looked back at the screen. The new scene presented her young self and Ryan in the small living area of their apartment several days after their engagement and first time making love. Chills streaked up and down Jill's spine. That day, and what had occurred, had been etched deep into her memory and had burned a lasting impression of sorrow on her emotional core. A lead ball of desperation thunked in her stomach. Being subjected to witness the travesty again disturbed her, especially since she had no control over the course of events and couldn't change anything.

The two of them had been so excited that week. The day after their engagement, Ryan had received the final interview call for a wonderful job opportunity in Philadelphia. He had been vying for the position with the fortune five hundred company for several weeks having gone on a couple preliminary interviews and submitting to a background check. The next interview would determine whether he was hired or not. If so, their future together would be financially set and allow them the means to have the life and family they wished. But then the day he had to travel the hour and a half into the city arrived and so had the hurricane.

The figures on the screen moved. Young Jill trailed after him as he wandered through the room looking for something.

"I still don't think you should go."

"Honey, look." Ryan stopped, turned and laid a hand on her shoulder. "What would the company think if I cancelled the interview because of a little rain? I'd loose this great opportunity."

"Little rain?" She flung her arm out to the side and pointed to the window. Sheets of water slid down the glass panes obscuring the view. "It's a torrential downpour. The weather reports aren't good. There's high winds, flooding, power outages. The radio said roads have washed away. There are hazardous downed electrical lines all over. They're also saying that people should stay off the streets. If you would only call and ask to postpone the interview, I'm sure they would understand. After all, the storm—"

Ryan pulled her into his arms and planted a quick kiss on her lips. "I'll be fine. I don't think they'd appreciate delaying their hiring process since they've recently been saying they need to make a decision as soon as possible. Plus, I'm leaving early. I'm giving myself plenty of time to take it easy and make it there safely."

She nuzzled her head against his chest. "I know you believe you'll be fine. I know they have a schedule to keep.

And I know it'd be a great opportunity for us, but I still can't shake this feeling that you shouldn't go."

"You worry too much. Perhaps you shouldn't listen to the news reports. All that negativity feeds your imagination and not in a good way."

"Please, Ryan. Please postpone." Young Jill hugged him tighter. "Please don't go."

"I have to." He pushed her a few inches away from him. "It'll be all right." Ryan pressed a few kisses along her jaw line, then made contact with her lips. It was a light teasing kiss, just enough to still her resistance. He trailed his hands down her arms, held her hands in his. He kissed her forehead and stepped back. "I love you."

"I love you, too."

He released her hands and picked up his briefcase. At the door he blew her a kiss. The click of the door closing seemed to boom in the small place.

The girl in the life film shivered, closed the sweater jacket she wore around her and hugged herself. She yawned and sat on the couch.

Older Jill squirmed in the theater seat. *I remember thinking there was a draft in the apartment. I had considered finding it, but once I sat down such a feeling of loneliness and despair took over that I took a nap to escape the feelings. I never did get a chance to find out if there was a draft or not.*

Time elapse flicked by in the movie jumping her to a few hours later after her short nap. Young Jill paced the small living room. The power had gone out. A small battery operated radio played from a spot on top of the television. News reports of the devastation the hurricane had caused filled the airways of all the stations. The announcers all harped on the same point. People should stay home, stay off the roadways. Several fatal accidents had happened on major highways all over the state.

Ryan hadn't called yet to say he made it to Philly.

She bit down on her nails. Her fingers had taken the brunt of her anxiousness and the areas around a few of her nail beds were red and swollen, bleeding from her teeth picking the skin.

A knock at the door startled her.

I had thought it might be our elderly neighbor, Ms. Wilkes, who liked to visit and chat when she was lonely. I had looked forward to the company, hoping it might take my mind off the storm. If I only I'd known…

Young Jill swung the door open and stopped short. Two police officers stood in the hall, their hats in their hands.

Older Jill cringed, unable to interfere, unable to stop the horror that was to come.

"Miss Norris?" the gentleman on the left inquired in a hesitant but polite voice.

"Yes?" Her gaze darted between the two people.

Panic and bile had risen in my throat.

"We were asked by the Ewingville Police Department to contact you. There was an accident at the Route 31 and I-95 interchange involving several cars. A Mr. Ryan Norn was in one of the vehicles. The officers on the scene found information on his person that noted you as his point of contact in case of emergency."

"Yes, he's my fiancé." Her breath hitched and her gaze swung to the policewoman. "Is he all right?"

I had to fight the urge to retch.

"Miss Norris," the woman stated slowly and sadly. "We regret to inform you the accident Mr. Norn was in proved fatal. He sustained major internal injuries and the medics on the scene couldn't revive him. His body is being held at R.W. Johnson Hospital. Is there anyone you would like us to help you call?"

Movie Jill stood frozen, a dumbfounded expression on her face.

Theater Jill continued to recall the surreal experience with clarity. *It had been like a plug had been pulled and my spirit had drained into the cosmos. I had the sensation of being completely empty, void of everything. I couldn't move, couldn't cry, couldn't scream. All my faculties had shut down, except for the crystal clear thoughts of what I had just been told.* Ryan was gone? No. It wasn't possible. The woman lied. *I had instantly grown numb in my denial and had functioned on auto-pilot.*

"Ma'am?"

On screen Jill blinked. She invited the officers in, handed them her address book and asked that they call his parents and hers. Once the calls were made, the officers assured her that their parents would be there soon. She stared at them, clamping her mouth shut. A muscle quivered at her jaw. Their words faded into the silence of the room. With somber expressions and a nod each, they left.

Alone, she crumpled to her knees. She beat the hardwood with her fists, shook her head like a mad woman.

I had railed against the world. Why had he decided to go? Why had fate taken him from me? What had happened was so unfair. Why did fate have to be so cruel?

Her young self on the screen threw her head back and screamed. The screech of anger eventually changed to a howl of sorrow.

Her old self sitting in the theater remembered the heart-wrenching wail. The grief in her reawakened. She wanted to wake up from the horrible dream.

"I should have tried harder to make him stay," the young Jill on the screen lamented.

"He should have decided to stay," older Jill stated, her voice furious at the inequitable dealings of fate.

"Should have, could have, and would have. Therein lays the hell of choices," Lady Tyche's voice mocked from somewhere high up in the darkened theater.

The young version of herself curled into a sobbing ball.

I had fallen into a deep black pit of wretchedness, experiencing a vicious cycle of denial, anger, and grief for days. When it got to the point where I couldn't cry anymore, and I had realized Ryan wouldn't ever walk back through the door again, I had climbed out of the thick despair into a bleak, gray existence. People thought I had finally accepted his death. But I don't believe I ever really did. The day he died, I had died, too.

Jill stood on shaky legs, staggered to the aisle, turned her back on the despondent woman on the screen, and with tottering steps, walked away. Tears streamed down her cheeks.

A month after the accident, her father had talked her into the first date with his associate Theodore Burke. Though she had said it was too soon, he'd worn her down. She eventually had acquiesced to her father's request. Her parents had wanted her to move on, to enjoy life again.

As a young woman, her decision to date in the midst of her grief and fall into a new love affair had turned out to be a good move. As an older woman looking back on that life changing event, she realized committing to Ted had been one of the worst things she had ever done.

After all, her precious Elsie, the only link she had left to Ryan, had turned out to be mean and callous, a disappointment. She was her father's daughter even though she wasn't biologically linked to Ted. Elsie would have been so different if Ryan had decided to stay home.

Chapter Seven

*J*ill opened the door to the theater and stepped into the great room of Lady Tyche's realm. The quest bag weighed down her shoulder. She surveyed the room to locate the lady and her consort.

The pair sat in a cozy embrace on the edge of the wheel. Ghostly figures huddled on the other side, far from the fate spinners.

She stomped over to the pair and dropped the bag at their feet.

The loud thud jerked Lady Tyche from her lip lock with *Herr* Sehend.

"I'm done with your quest. Here are your items. Now return me to where I belong," Jill demanded, exhaustion nipping at every pore and strand of muscle in her body.

Lady Tyche hopped off the wheel. She helped her companion down. He whispered in her ear, shooting Jill a devious glare.

"I have decided I shall not send you back." The tall graceful lady flipped a hand in the air, laughed and spun the wheel. She took the hand of her blindfolded servant and led him to a pair of thrones. After they sat, she leaned over and kissed him.

Cocking her head, Jill tried to understand what had just happened. Had Lady Tyche blown her off? Was she truly not going home? She gritted her teeth and fought down the snarl of anger threatening to choke her. How dare that woman renege on her promise! She stormed over to the woman who continued to play tonsil hockey.

"I command you to send me home!"

The kiss ended abruptly. Lady Tyche turned, tilted her head and glared at her. "You command me?" She rose with a ramrod straight back. "You dare presume to command me to do as you bid? I should—"

Herr Sehend tugged on her dress.

"Yes? What is it?" She snapped as she turned and looked at him. He motioned for her to come close to him. She bent forward, and he whispered in her ear. When she righted, her gaze ignored Jill and focused on the wheel. "Ah, my sweet, you are right." Still disregarding Jill, she took his hand and led him back to the wheel.

Jill spun, her gaze narrowed on their backs, galled at their blatant snub and followed them.

A new ghost sat on the wheel, its spectral facial expression filled with fright. Lady Tyche and her man put their hands on the spokes and pushed the wheel into a spin.

Frustrated over her mistreatment, Jill rushed the wheel and grabbed on to a spoke. She dug her heels into the ground and leaned back, throwing her weight into stopping the cycle. The wispy figure jerked to and fro, and fell off. The chorus lining the walls of the grand room laughed at the ghost's tumble.

"How dare you," Lady Tyche bellowed. She whirled around, focusing her wrath on Jill, her stare blazing with ire. "What nerve you have stopping my wheel! It is not your duty to decide fate."

"It's not your job either to *personally* decide one's fate," she roared back, tired of the games, tired of being where she was, tired of being her. "It's the wheel's job."

Lady Tyche waved her hands and arms in the air in irritation. "Fine. We shall let the wheel decide whether you stay here in my realm or you go back to where you came." She clapped her hands twice. The smoky figures vanished from the area. Without the help of *Herr* Sehend, she pushed the wheel with the force of both of her arms and body.

The circular contraption rotated at a dizzying speed. Jill said a silent prayer of thanks that Lady Tyche hadn't made her ride it. The clicking slowed. The wheel decelerated more. All was quiet in the room save for the dwindling flaps of the flipper against the posts. The wheel came to a complete stop and no one made a sound.

A faint gasp sounded from the south end of the room and was followed by another. Everyone's heads turned to the lion's corner. Jill's gaze flitted from one member of the chorus to another and finally followed where all the stares led.

A man stood in the place of the lion statue. A tall, gorgeous man with a full head of blond hair and a body of a swimmer.

Ryan!

Jill's heart lifted in joy and her body sloughed off its extreme fatigue. She ran to Ryan, flung her arms around him and kissed her way along his jaw line. She crushed her mouth to his in a kiss of wild abandon, the taste and feel of him spilling through to her soul. Jill poured everything she was into the kiss, not wanting to let go. A chill streaked through her body when she thought about losing him again.

He pushed her a few inches away from him. "It'll be all right." Ryan pressed several kisses along her jaw line, then made contact with her lips. It was a light teasing kiss, just enough to still her resistance. He trailed his hands down her arms, held her hands in his. He kissed her forehead and stepped back. "I love you."

"I love you, too."

I love you, too? A distinct sense of *déjà vu* stole over her. She glanced around her. The scenery had changed. She was back in the old apartment. *No! Not again!*

"Baby, what's wrong?" Ryan asked, releasing her hands and picking up his briefcase. "You look confused."

"I thought," she paused and shook her head. She thought her quest was through, but how could she explain that to him?

"Never mind." And as much as it pained her to say it, she added, "You better get going."

At the door he blew her a kiss. The click of the door as it shut seemed to boom in the small place and echo through her primal essence.

She sat on the couch, but no sense of despair or utter loneliness followed.

The door opened and Ryan stepped back inside. "I forgot my watch." His gaze darted around the room and landed on the small table near the kitchenette. "Ah, there it is." He hurried over to the table and grabbed it.

The phone shrilled.

Baffled over the change in events, Jill stayed rooted on the couch. Ryan threw her a puzzled look, walked over to where the phone hung on the wall next to the fridge and answered it.

A muffled voice sounded through the handset. While the person on the other end spoke, Ryan opened his briefcase, pulled out his day planner and flipped through a few pages.

"Sure, next Tuesday will be fine. Yes, barring any more inclement weather. I'm looking forward to it. You too. Thanks for your call." He hung up the phone. A bright smile lit his face. He shucked his overcoat and tossed it onto a chair. "Well, babe, that was Mr. Etaf on the phone. They said they're delaying the interviews due to the hurricane. They want their future employees to be safe. So you got your wish. I'm staying home. Safe and sound and, since I have the afternoon free, hopefully in your arms."

Jill rose from the couch still unsure of what was happening. *This wasn't how that day went. What am I supposed to do?* With tentative steps she walked toward Ryan catching her reflection in the mirror near the door along the way. A youthful visage stared back.

Your quest is over. You're back at the beginning, Lady Tyche's voice stated in a whisper in her mind. *Until we meet again, use the wisdom you've gained and remember to make wise decisions.*

"Honey?"

The concern in Ryan's question brought her out of her deep thoughts. She skipped over to him and wrapped her arms around him, feeling his strength, his warmth, his life.

"Thank God you're not going. You don't know how happy this makes me."

He kissed the top of her head and rested his cheek there. "You know, now that I think about it, I'm glad I don't have to go. At least not today. Though I have a great feeling about the position, driving to the interview in this weather kind of concerned me."

"It concerned me and the little one, too."

"Little one?"

She stepped out of his arms, placed her hands on her abdomen and nodded her head. "I'm not one hundred percent certain yet because it's way too soon for a test, but I have strong hunch we created a baby the other night. I debated whether I should tell you before or after the interview and had decided on after. I didn't want it clouding your mind while you were trying to make a good impression. I planned to cook your favorite meal, and when you got home, we'd eat. Then I was going to give you the news. I have a strong suspicion you're going to be a daddy."

Ryan cheered, swept her up in his arms and spun. "That's wonderful! You're sure about this?"

"Pretty confident." Images of an alternate life, one that included a child, flickered in her mind. "Call it a woman's intuition. We'll find out definitely in a few weeks. I hope that's okay."

"It's more than okay." He put her back on her feet and gave her a squeeze. "It's great. God, I love you Jill. So does this female sixth sense tell you whether the baby is a boy or a girl?"

"A girl. A beautiful baby girl."

Ryan wrapped his arms around her again. "A princess for my queen."

෴෴෴෴

Tears of joy streamed from Jill's eyes. She wouldn't end up in a loveless marriage, and her and Ryan's darling baby girl wouldn't be raised and influenced by a greedy, self-centered cad.

Happiness for her new way of life and the fresh start filled her. Jill offered up silent gratitude to Lady Fortune. She was back in the arms of her love.

෴෴෴෴

ABOUT THE AUTHOR

An eccentric and eclectic writer, C.R. Moss pens stories for the mainstream and erotic markets, giving readers Worlds of Possibilities when it comes to love and romance. For more about the woman behind the keyboard, visit: http://www.crmoss.net/Author.htm